PUFFIN BOOKS
STORM BIRD

On 9 July 1905 Jenny Lovatt's comfortable world falls apart: her father's grocery business is ruined, and the only way he can support the two of them is by returning with her to his birthplace – the East Anglian fishing village of Newbrigg – and to the sea. For Jenny this means an uncertain future under the care of her Aunt Clara, a woman who, she discovers, is difficult and at times frightening.

But fortunately she is befriended by Josh Gale, son of the wealthy brewery owners. Small and shy, his driving ambition, despite fierce opposition from his father, is to be an ornithologist and there is no danger he will not face in order to fulfil his dream.

Finding mutual friendship and solace, Jenny becomes a collaborator in Josh's dangerous secret life. With her father away at sea, she also finds herself increasingly involved in the mysteries that surround her Aunt Clara's past, gradually uncovering the tangled web of horror and tragedy that haunts the whole of Newbrigg. As she is to discover, the torment is far from over.

Elsie McCutcheon is married with a grown-up daughter and lives in Suffolk. Formerly an English teacher, she has a great interest in local history and is addicted to buying second-hand books. *Summer of the Zeppelin*, also a Puffin book, was runner-up for the *Guardian* Award in 1983.

S0-AFN-084

Storm Bird

Elsie McCutcheon

PUFFIN BOOKS

PUFFIN BOOKS

Published by the Penguin Group
27 Wrights Lane, London W8 5TZ, England
Viking Penguin Inc., 40 West 23rd Street, New York, New York 10010, USA
Penguin Books Australia Ltd, Ringwood, Victoria, Australia
Penguin Books Canada Ltd, 2801 John Street, Markham, Ontario, Canada L3R 1B4
Penguin Books (NZ) Ltd, 182–190 Wairau Road, Auckland 10, New Zealand

Penguin Books Ltd, Registered Offices: Harmondsworth, Middlesex, England

First published by J. M. Dent 1987
Published in Puffin Books 1988
1 3 5 7 9 10 8 6 4 2

Printed and bound in Great Britain by
Cox & Wyman Ltd, Reading
Filmset in Bembo

For
Heather and Lorraine Dick
and
Clare and Alistair Glover

Chapter 1

The bird flew in from the sea. It alighted on the roof of the salt-store, the brick building on the quay nearest the river. The ridge-tiles had been pleasantly warmed by the mild September sun and the bird, having flapped its wings twice, settled down to preen contentedly. It was a roller – a handsome specimen: green-headed, with a pinky-chestnut back and wings of turquoise and azure like the sea behind it. A week ago nature had played it a dirty trick, injecting it with the sudden futile urge to leave its home above Lake Como and fly westward. It was forty years since one of its kind had done likewise – only to find a permanent roost in Newbrigg Museum where it still stared glassily across the room at a case of dusty eagles and owls.

But this bird, whose round, bright eyes now looked down on the clumps of parasols, the yachting-caps and the multi-coloured prize flags fluttering on the rigging of anchored yachts, seemed unaware that it might be in danger. All at once it launched itself from the roof, made a wide circle over the river, climbed, then began to somersault, tumbling over and over in a whirl of flame, emerald and blue. Josh Gale, leading the one-designs home, happened to look upwards just at that moment and saw the bird – with disastrous consequences.

Josh had had a good race after a precarious start, when his dinghy, *Galaxy*, had hung uncertainly in the wind for what had seemed an eternity before her sail filled. The first and third legs had been to windward and he had taken the lead after the last turn. Although the tide was on the ebb, this final leg home had been a fast one with the wind in their favour and, seeing the finishing line a bare forty yards away, Josh held his head up and smiled. He knew that his father would be watching him through his binoculars from the committee-boat, so he must look as though he had enjoyed being drenched by spray and flayed and half-deafened by the wind. His father genuinely believed that you were bound to enjoy sailing if you were a Gale, that it was an inherited trait like the Gales' long second toe. Last year, when Josh had turned down the chance of competing solo in the regatta for the first time, Mr Gale had looked as dismayed and astounded as though his only son had suddenly announced he no longer believed in God.

Since last September, however, Josh had learned to be diplomatic – sometimes even plain cunning. It was the one useful skill he had brought away with him from Shrublands House. Small for his age, and fond of his own company, he had had to outwit or appease the school bullies – and sometimes the masters too. It was strategy that had freed him from his prison last May – he had lain out on the school's leads one cold spring night to worsen a heavy cold and had ended up with a patch on his lung. Now, since he seemed perfectly healthy again, he had to keep in his father's good books so that Mr Gale would not renege on his agreement with Dr Buchan to keep Josh at home under parental supervision for at least a year.

For the time being, however, Josh was being given lessons five mornings a week by Mr Hanley, the curate. It was an arrangement which suited him well, for it left the afternoons free for his ornithology. "It's not just bird-watching! Not just a hobby! It can be a real profession," he used to cry hotly during arguments with his father about his future. But that had been before Shrublands House. Now he knew better than to argue. He kept quiet about his plan to become an ornithologist and his determination not, on any account, to go into the family brewery. Hidden, his resolve grew daily stronger.

Meanwhile, Josh had to placate his father and convince him that an eleven-year-old boy was not necessarily a muff because he was not away at school. 'Muff' was a word Mr Gale used frequently to describe anyone who was lacking in ability and courage and could not stand on his own feet. This was why Josh had decided he must show himself a winner by taking the cup for the one-design race in this year's regatta. After all, although he disliked sailing, he had had nine years' experience, having been carried aboard his grandfather's cutter for his first trip when he was just two years old. What Josh lacked when sailing, as his father was always telling him, was concentration. He would fall into a daydream as he put down the helm for instance, then suddenly find that the boat had stopped dead and the sail was flapping hopelessly like a caged bird.

Today, however, he had kept his mind on the task in hand, judging the gusts of wind nicely, never allowing the tiller in his left hand, or the sheet in his right, to move or slip from his control even a fraction.

"Reckon they're goin' to make a sailor of that lad yet," Lucky Fulcher, the wiry little master of Mr Gale's yacht, remarked to the quay in general. He jumped up from the bollard on which he had been sitting and spat a gobbet of tobacco in a triumphant arc out into the river.

On board the committee-boat, Wilfred Gale lowered his binoculars and tried to hide his gratification at the sight of his son running home so easily at least fifteen yards ahead of the second dinghy. The boy was turning out well after all. He might be puny-looking and have a peculiar obsession about birds, but he was a true Gale. He had handled the race masterfully.

"Yes. Not bad. Not bad," he admitted modestly as other committee-members called out their congratulations.

But, barely a moment later, Josh looked up and saw the tumbling bird. "Crikey!" he exclaimed. He half stood up, leaning over the gunwale. "It can't be! Is it . . ? It is . . ! It's a roller! A blue roller!" In his excitement he lifted both hands to shade his eyes against the sun. The *Galaxy*, uncontrolled, sheered wildly and swept round towards the committee-boat.

Lucky Fulcher, on the quay, gave a wail of despair, took off his cap and banged it again and again on his knee.

"Josh!" yelled Mr Gale. "Josh! What the blazes?"

"You're a-goin' to gybe, lad! Look out for yerself!" Lucky roared.

The warning came too late. Even as Fulcher shouted, the *Galaxy*'s sail and boom went over with an almighty jerk, Josh was sent flying into the water and the dinghy capsized. As the whistle shrilled out for the rescue-boat, the boy climbed agilely up over the *Galaxy*'s gunwale to sit with legs astride. Then he gazed upwards again at the bird which was still gliding, climbing and somersaulting overhead. A smile of perfect happiness lit his face.

Josh was oblivious to his father watching him, standing apart from his friends in his moment of humiliation and gripping the rail of the boat so tightly that his knuckles showed ivory. Josh saw nothing but the miraculous acrobatic tumbling of the exuberant roller. Then a gun went off for another race and the bird took fright, climbing high before turning to the west and heading upriver towards Wenford.

Chapter 2

A quarter of an hour later Jenny Lovett spied the roller. By then it was perched on the mast of a schooner which was lying at anchor in midstream. The train had been stationary at Wenford Halt for several minutes and Jenny was standing with her warm forehead pressed against the carriage window, gazing out at the mudflats and the anchored barges. There were a lot of black-and-white birds on the mud, sitting in little bunches or stalking around at the edge of the water, probing with their bills. Seagulls, she assumed – though in fact they were different kinds of waders. Then, suddenly, she looked up and saw the roller. Even at a distance its colours were distinct and vibrant. Knowing little about birds, and recognizing with certainty only the sparrows, robins and blackbirds that had come to the garden of their north London terrace house, Jenny thought it must be a kind of parrot. It probably belongs to the schooner's captain, she decided, or perhaps to one of the crew. She could imagine it sitting on a sailor's shoulder, squawking. She turned to tell her father about it, but he was still asleep. There was no one else left now in their third-class compartment. After a moment she sighed rather tremulously and sat down again.

Tall, well-built and with a naturally solemn expression, Jenny looked older than her twelve years. And, since her father's troubles had started, she had had to behave as though she were older too. This was difficult at times. It was especially difficult today when she was feeling miserable about leaving Latimer Gardens, where she had been born, and nervous about meeting Aunt Clara whom she had never seen before. But Mrs Harris had said Jenny must try to be brave for her father's sake. On that Sunday evening two months ago – 9 July 1905 – when they had learned from the wholesaler's man, Mr Robinson, about Arthur Gillybrand's embezzling Dad's money, Mrs Harris had gripped Jenny's shoulders with her red, rheumaticky old hands and said, "You'll have to be a woman now, Jen. I'll do my best to help him. But I'm only the housekeeper. You'll have to support him the way your mother would have done. So no grumbling or self-pity."

"You warned him about Mr Gillybrand from the very beginning," Jenny said tearfully. "You never liked him. Why didn't he listen?" They were in the kitchen, talking softly like conspirators, although Mr Lovett had dashed out ten minutes before to catch the nine o'clock horse-bus which would take him almost to Gillybrand's gate.

"Och, he was taken in by the man's guile," replied Mrs Harris, turning away to wring out a dishcloth in the sink as viciously as though it were Gillybrand's fat neck. "Your dad's a trusting man. But then maybe I've met a few more villains in my day than he has."

Not that Mrs Harris had ever dreamed that Gillybrand was the villain he turned out to be. On that dreadful night of the ninth of July, when Mr Lovett finally arrived home at eleven o'clock with his grim news, her face turned ashen.

"He admits he has spent all your money. Bold as brass. Oh, the rogue! The devil!" she said in a trembling voice. "But what will you do, Mr Lovett? Whatever will you do?" She put an arm round Jenny who had insisted on waiting up for her father's return.

"I can't prosecute. I haven't a leg to stand on. It was my own negligence. But I'll pay off every penny I owe," Mr Lovett replied, leaning wearily against the mantelshelf. "I've walked all the way home so that I could think it out. Folks can say I was a fool, Mrs Harris. But they'll never say I was a dishonest fool. It will be the finish of the business, I reckon. But I can always go back to the sea."

"Leave London?" Jenny cried in dismay, and felt Mrs Harris squeeze her shoulder reprovingly.

"Just for a year, poppet," her father said, trying to smile. "Just until I've made enough for a fresh start. A good winter's fishing and a summer's yachting should see us all right. We'll go home to Newbrigg. Your Aunt Clara will take us in." He turned to the elderly housekeeper and shrugged helplessly. "Mrs Harris," he started, his voice cracking for the first time, "I'm sorry. But I can't . . . ."

"Don't you trouble yourself about me," Mrs Harris broke in briskly. "I can go to my single brother in Glasgow. He'll be glad of me to fetch and carry for him. But there!" she finished in a brighter tone. "Maybe we're looking on the black side, Mr Lovett. The position might not be as bad as you think."

It had been every bit as bad, though. The following day Mr Lovett had discovered that, thanks to Gillybrand, he owed a great deal of money, not just to one but four wholesalers. Almost everything they owned had had to be sold off. The shop. Its stock. Even their furniture. It had taken Mr Lovett two months to put his affairs in order.

A whistle blew and the train jumped nervously. It moved

6

forward in a series of jerks, then settled into a steady rhythm. The schooner, the bird that Jenny thought was a parrot, the barges and the waders all slid away, and in their place were flat, empty fields criss-crossed by ditches. "Pieces of eight, pieces of eight," chanted the train.

Even under the tranquil blue sky of a fine September day the landscape looked melancholy to Jenny. All that emptiness without people or houses! What would it be like in winter, she wondered with a shiver. And would Newbrigg be equally desolate? Then she remembered that Newbrigg was a seaside town and a holiday resort, and she decided it must surely look livelier than this.

"Going to live at the seaside!" Mrs Harris had said when the decision had been taken. "Och, but you're a lucky girl, Jen. I always dreamed of living by the sea. In a wee but-and-ben on the Firth of Clyde maybe. And what happened to me? At twenty-five I met Mr Harris and exchanged the dust of Glasgow for the dust of London. And now I'm seventy and it's back to Glasgow again."

Jenny would not willingly have left her London home for anywhere else on earth. It seemed to her that she had always been blissfully happy there. She had no memories of her mother, who had died when Jenny was two. But with Mrs Harris and her father to look after her she had never wanted for care or affection.

At Laurel Park Elementary she had met Mary Moore who soon became her best friend and was always her rival for the position at the top of the class. Next June, Mary and Jenny were to have sat the Cambridge Local Exam for places at Woodside Girls Upper School. Miss Grant, their favourite teacher, had said they were both clever enough to remain at school until they were eighteen, and perhaps win a scholarship to a university. Jenny had had a letter from Miss Grant last week saying how sorry she was to be losing her. "But I'm sure you will be a credit to Laurel Park and will do just as well in your Suffolk schools as you have done here," she had finished.

What was Mary doing at this moment? Jenny wondered.

Suddenly she had to swallow hard. Why had that hateful man, Gillybrand, turned up to ruin everything? Dad had had to work very hard in his little corner shop, but he had always seemed to enjoy it. "Your mother would have been real proud to see a thriving little business like we have now," he had told Jenny on his birthday last October. "The shop was her idea, you know, after I'd followed her to London to ask her to marry me. She was working as nursemaid then for the Langton-Birketts, the family she had come to Newbrigg with that summer."

It was shortly after this conversation that Arthur Gillybrand appeared on the scene. Mr Lovett had met him at the local traders' social club and within two weeks he had agreed to take Gillybrand into the shop and let him run a newspaper-and-stationery side.

And that was the end of Lovett's shop, Jenny thought bleakly. Yesterday, 15 September, she and her father had gone to Euston Station to see Mrs Harris safely on her journey to Glasgow. This morning their remaining furniture had gone to the saleroom in a horse and cart. And at half-past ten Mr Lovett had turned the key in the front door of 32 Latimer Gardens for the last time. Neighbours, customers, and friends had gathered at the gate to shake their hands and wish them good luck. Some had walked to the bus-stop with them. They all wanted Mr Lovett to know that they admired him for what he had done, and Jenny felt proud, as though she were in a triumphal procession. Not until the train was steaming out of Liverpool Street Station did the reaction set in, her heart suddenly feeling stone-heavy as it dawned on her how much she was leaving behind.

Mr Lovett choked on a snore and opened his eyes. For a moment he stared at Jenny blankly. Then he found his bearings. "I must have dropped off for a few minutes," he said, yawning and stretching.

"You've been asleep since we left Colchester," Jenny informed him.

"Where are we now then?" asked her father. "Near Ipswich yet?" He half rose from his seat to look through the window. Then his eyes widened. "Well! I'll go to the devil!" he exclaimed. "Why didn't you wake me up, Jen? We're nearly at Newbrigg. We're just passing the North Marsh. Look at all those birds!" Hundreds of birds had flown up in alarm from a wide green marsh dotted with little pools. Through this living curtain Jenny could see a band of blue.

"The sea!" she cried excitedly, shuffling along the seat to press her nose against the window. Her spirits lifted. She had never imagined that the North Sea would be blue like the sea at Broadstairs, where she and Mrs Harris spent a week every summer. She had thought of it always as grey with angry white wave-tops.

"Yes. She's smiling today," Mr Lovett remarked as he pulled their two suitcases down from the rack. "But you'll see her in a different mood soon. Come October she'll be piling up her great high tides and rampaging over the prom."

Woods and fields slid past quite slowly now. A cottage came into view and, through its open door, Jenny saw a woman smack the hand of a child who was reaching up to a table. A signal-box, then a platform crawled by. Waiting-rooms. A bookstall. The train inched along, then stopped with a jerk.

"Newbrigg!" a porter hollered.

Mr Lovett opened the compartment door.

"Fish!" exclaimed Jenny, wrinkling her nose at the strong smell wafting over from a pile of empty boxes against the wall.

"You'll have to get used to that," her father told her as she jumped down on to the platform beside him.

He hurried her out of the small station, keeping his cap pulled low over his eyes as he handed their tickets to the collector at the gate. He doesn't feel like talking yet, or answering their questions, Jenny thought. And she suddenly

9

realized how painful it must be for her father to be returning to Newbrigg down on his luck. She wished she could take his arm, but he was carrying a large suitcase in each hand.

When they came out of the station-yard they turned right. "We'll take the back way," said Mr Lovett. "It's quicker than going down through the town."

"Wall Road," observed Jenny as they passed the name-plate on the corner. She knew this was where Aunt Clara lived, so she stared in some surprise at the grand-looking villas with their turrets and carriage drives and extensive front lawns. They might have been in one of the high-class London sub-urbs, had it not been for the tingling smell of the sea.

"Longest road in Newbrigg," her father said as he strode on. "This is the end where the nobs live. Incomers most of them. All kinds too. Writers. Scientists. Explorers. We're bound for the far end and the ordinary mortals."

"I thought Aunt Clara might have met us," said Jenny a few minutes later. She was a little out of breath, for she was having to keep up with her father's brisk pace.

Mr Lovett smiled down at her uneasily. "About your Aunt Clara, poppet," he said. "You might find her a bit cold to begin with. Abrupt. Don't be put off by first impressions. She has a heart of gold underneath. But don't ask her any questions about her young days, Jen. She doesn't like that. Remember, now."

Jenny began to feel queasy with nerves. She wished now that her father had brought her to Newbrigg on visits so that at least she would have known what lay in store for her. He could have brought her after Grandmother Lovett died, when he had gone to the funeral and made his peace with Aunt Clara, his adopted sister.

Jenny had been seven when her father's mother had died. (Her mother had been an orphan, brought up in a home, so she had no maternal grandparents.) She had heard all about the rift then between her father and his family. How the Lovetts had quarrelled with Dad because he had preferred Jenny's mother and his London corner shop to a share in the family fishing-

boat along with his father and his younger brother, Alfred.
How they had blamed Jenny's mother, Rosa, for taking Dad
away from them, and had not even come up to London to see
him when Rosa died giving birth to a stillborn boy. Then
Grandfather Lovett and Alfred had both been drowned in 1898
when their fishing-smack had been lying to in a gale. Alfred
had been pulling the net in when a heavy sea had hit and
washed him overboard, and Grandfather, making a grab for
him, had slipped on the deck and fallen in too. Grandmother
Lovett had written to tell him the details of the tragedy, but
had said she did not wish him to come to the funeral service.
She herself had developed heart trouble shortly afterwards and
had spent the last year of her life a bedridden invalid, nursed by
Aunt Clara. After her funeral, Christmas cards and an occasional letter came to 32 Latimer Gardens from Aunt Clara in
Newbrigg. But Jenny had never even seen a photograph of her
aunt and knew little about her except that she was very
religious.

Mr Lovett was walking more slowly now, his shoulders
drooping, his boots kicking against stones on the dusty,
unsurfaced road, because he was too tired to pick up his feet.

"Can't I carry one of the cases?" she asked, looking up at
him anxiously. She thought of him as quite old. Thirty-nine
on his next birthday. What if he had a heart-attack?

"Too heavy for you," he told her. "But we haven't far to go
now. See that bend? Well, it's all downhill from there."

They passed some empty tennis courts with a board on the
gate saying, *Private. Members Only*. "We haven't seen a single
soul since we turned into Wall Road," Jenny pointed out.

"That's because it's Regatta Day," said her father. "Everyone's down at the river. This is the most important day of the
year in Newbrigg. I met your mother on Regatta Day, 1890."
Now that they were going downhill he was swinging along
again.

Jenny skipped by his side. He had told her a hundred times
the story of how he had met her mother, but she never tired of
hearing it.

11

"She was standing on the quay, wasn't she?" she prompted. "With the Langton–Birkett baby in its perambulator and the little girl by her side."

"The prettiest young woman you ever saw," said her father. "Hair the colour of ripe wheat and a green dress of some flimsy stuff."

"And then didn't the baby throw its toy lamb into the river?"

"That's right. And you've never seen such a rush as there was to rescue that little old toy," chuckled Mr Lovett. "Boats came from all directions. All the eligible bachelors in New-brigg rowing like the devil. But the best man won."

They were almost at the foot of the hill now, and some way ahead on the right Jenny could see a red-brick terrace. She was about to ask her father if that was where they were bound for, when he stopped and nodded towards a large white house with bay windows on the other side of the road. It had a fine cedar tree in the centre of its lawn.

"Look, Jen," he said. "Galaxy House. That belongs to the Gale family who have the big brewery in Wenford. Your Aunt Clara works for them as daily cook. She started there at fourteen as scullery-maid. That was twenty-one years ago."

Before he could say any more two figures appeared, walking very rapidly towards them along the centre of the road. Or, to be more exact, the smaller of the two, a boy, was having to trot to keep up with the long strides of a man dressed in white trousers, a navy jacket and a yachting-cap. From the distance, Jenny thought the man, who had a white moustache and a bronzed face, looked very handsome. But, as the pair drew nearer, she could see that he was scowling unpleasantly and could hear his grating voice as he berated the boy. Man and boy passed through the gateway of Galaxy House without a glance in Jenny's and her father's direction.

"That was Mr Gale. The lad must be his son – the tail-ender. He was the little surprise bundle that came along years after his sisters," Mr Lovett informed Jenny.

"Well, his father doesn't look exactly doting," commented

12

Jenny. She felt an unaccountable rush of sympathy for the skinny little boy with the hangdog look.

"No. Not today at any rate," agreed Mr Lovett. Then he lifted the cases which he had set down at his feet. "Come on," he said. "Let's go and see Clara. Number Five in Mariners Terrace yonder. Those houses opposite the field with the horses in it. Middle of the row we are. Sandwiched between the Blocks on one side and old Mrs Fulcher on the other. Wonder what Clara will say when she sees you?"

Chapter 3

In fact, when she opened the door to Mr Lovett's knock, Aunt Clara said nothing at all. A slight woman, not much taller than Jenny, with a sallow complexion, prominent brown eyes and dark hair pulled severely back from her forehead, she merely smiled and nodded before ushering them along a dark little passage to the kitchen, where three places were set at a scrubbed deal table. In the centre of the table was a plate of scones, a sponge cake and a tray of shortbread.

"Well, what's all this?" cried Mr Lovett, shoving the two suitcases into the corner behind the door. "You wicked girl, Clara Lovett! Didn't I say you mustn't go to any trouble? Reckon you've enough to do up at Galaxy House."

"That weren't much trouble, Edward. Glad to be bakin' for my own folk again." Aunt Clara's voice was as small and pinched as herself. She had backed against the dresser and was rubbing her hands up and down her white apron, her eyes darting nervously between Mr Lovett and Jenny.

Looking at her, Jenny felt her apprehensions vanish. Not a Clara was quite different to how she had imagined her. Not a dragon at all, but a plain, shy little spinster.

"I'm pleased to meet you, Aunt Clara," she said, walking forward confidently and offering her hand.

"Pleased to meet you, too, I'm sure." Cold fingers brushed Jenny's for a moment. "An' now I'll be infusin' the tea, do you want to pay a visit, or wash yer hands. We got piped water since you was last here, Edward, along o' three summer visitors catchin' fever . . . Go through the scullery an' you'll see the back door, my mawther."

Jenny went out and hurried down the long, narrow back garden between the rows of cabbages and currant bushes, not because she needed to visit the lavatory urgently, but because she wanted to know the worst. She sighed with relief when she opened the green door, caught a strong whiff of disinfectant, and saw the spotless whitewashed walls with a framed notice on the left-hand one informing her that cleanliness was next to godliness. Ever since Mr Lovett had warned Jenny that Aunt Clara had an outside lavatory, she had been envisaging the kind of dark, evil-smelling closet, rat and insect-ridden, that some of her less fortunate schoolmates had had in their backyards. In this one, however, there was not even a spider's web to be seen.

When she returned to the kitchen she found her father turning over some garments that had been laid out on the dresser. He was looking as pleased as a small boy with his Christmas presents. Jenny guessed immediately that this was the gear about which he had been worrying – the clothes he would need for a season's fishing. There were tan jumpers, finely knitted navy guernseys, thick white jerseys and long blue boot-stockings. Beneath the dresser was a suit of new yellow oilskins and a short and a long pair of seaboots. Aunt Clara, he said, had bought these for him and had sewed the jumpers and knitted the woollies. She must have started work on them as soon as she received Dad's first letter telling her of his misfortune, Jenny thought.

"I'll pay you back just as soon as I'm able to, Clara," Mr Lovett said gruffly, patting his sister on the shoulder.

"I don't want paid back, I'm sure," Aunt Clara muttered. She lifted the big black kettle from the range and carried it over to the table to refill the pot, from which three cups of tea had been poured. Her cheeks were pink, though whether from leaning over the fire, or from embarrassment, Jenny could not tell.

"Sit you down together then," she told them abruptly. "Don't matter where. An' perhaps you'll say grace, Edward."

Jenny chose the chair with its back to the window and facing the dresser. Beside the latter hung a framed sampler which read, *God is Master in this House*. And, beneath, in small letters, *Worked by Clara Lovett. April 1881*. Jenny's father sat down opposite her and Aunt Clara sat at the end of the table with her back to the range. While her father was saying, "For what we are about to receive," Jenny's half-closed left eye spied another framed text above the mantelshelf which reminded her that she must not forget to keep the Sabbath Day holy. According to her father, Aunt Clara kept it exceptionally holy and no one in the house was allowed to wash a dish, or even sew on a button. Jenny did not mind that, but she would mind not being allowed to read her books which had been packed away at the bottom of her trunk.

Aunt Clara began to hand round the plates and, as though she had read Jenny's mind, said, "Yer trunks come last Thursday, Edward. I had the man carry them both up to the back bedroom. Jenny can sleep in there. An' you can have the front bedroom till you leave. Mrs Gale's loaned me a foldin' bed I can put up in here."

"Well, I'll have that," declared Mr Lovett. "I'm not putting you out of your room, Clara. I might be weeks finding a boat to take me on."

"Shouldn't think so," said Aunt Clara with an enigmatic smile.

Mr Lovett stared at her for a moment. Then, "Clara Lovett!" he cried. "You've heard of a berth. Haven't you, now? Own up, girl!"

She shot him a teasing look from beneath her black brows. "I'm keepin' the good news for afters, Edward," she said. "Have yer tea first. Then, when we've shown young Jenny over the house – an' that won't take long, as you know – then you'll hear!"

Mr Lovett knew there was no point in protesting, for Clara was not really the mouse she appeared. There was a deep stubborn streak in her, which became more pronounced the older she grew. For instance, nothing would induce her to work on a Sunday, not all Mr Gale's cajoling, or Mrs Gale's veiled threats of finding another, more amenable, cook. So, if Clara wanted to withhold her news for another half-hour, his becoming impatient or irritated would not change her mind. He nodded resignedly, therefore, helped himself to a piece of sponge cake, and gave Jenny a surreptitious wink.

Jenny was thinking that it was all turning out much better than she had feared. No dragon-aunt. No horrid outside lavatory. And not even Mrs Harris could have found fault with this sparkling kitchen, with its woodwork scrubbed to the colour of butter, and the brass candlesticks, pewter dishes and copper jelly-moulds on the dresser glinting in the sunlight.

Aunt Clara saw Jenny's roving eye. "Them lines round the walls. That's not dirt, you know," she said. "No. Those is tide-marks left when we've bin flooded. Can't get rid of them nohow. Three coats of whitewash I've put on since the last flood, but them old lines still show through. That annoy me some, Edward. I'd wholly like one of them new houses up on the hill by the church, out of the way of the sea. I could have wallpaper then. Wallpaper don't fare to stick on these walls at all now, they got so damp."

Jenny felt her stomach somersault as she looked up at the greenish-black line which she had not noticed until that moment. Even if she stood up it would be at least eighteen inches above her head! The shock of Aunt Clara's revelation made her feel quite weak and she put her cup down abruptly on her saucer. She stared accusingly at her father. He ought to have warned her about the floods. She might have worried, but at least she would have had time to come to terms with the idea! Jenny did not know it, but her face had turned the colour of the floury scones on the table.

"Clara!" Mr Lovett was half-laughing, half-concerned.

16

"You've scared Jenny out of her wits. She thinks she's going to be drowned by the next high tide."

"Drownded?" Aunt Clara sounded mystified that anyone should be worried about the sea suddenly filling their house to within six inches of the roof. She shook her head. "I never known anyone to be drownded in the floods, have you, Edward? Soon as the old sea start comin' over the green, they come an' warn you. That give you time to git' yer good furniture upstairs on to the landin', an' to move out yerself if you want to. Clearin' up afterwards, that's the nightmare. Six barrerloads of shingle I had in here last time. An' the mud! That were suffin' chronic."

"I wasn't hiding it from you, Jen," said Mr Lovett. "I just forgot to mention it. If you grow up beside the North Sea you take high tides and flooding for granted. They're part of the winter. Like a London fog."

"I'd rather have fogs than floods," said Jenny. But she felt much happier. As long as she was not in danger of being drowned she would not mind helping to move the furniture upstairs, or to clear out the shingle and mud.

Aunt Clara had turned round several times to look at the clock on the mantelshelf. She did so again now and, seeing that it was half-past five, gave a vexed "Tut-tut".

"How time do fly!" she observed with a sigh. "I got to leave you at six to go up to the House an' make a start on their dinner. They're havin' a party tonight."

Mr Lovett was on his feet right away. "Come on, Jen," he cried. "We mustn't keep Clara back. She wants to show you your room. And then she has something to tell me."

"Ah! You ain't forgot that then, Edward." Aunt Clara's head went down and she giggled.

"You know very well I haven't, girl!"

"Well, afore we go up aloft, come an' have a look at the parlour."

They followed her along the passage to the front room.

"My!" said Mr Lovett, looking round with approval. "This is tasteful, Clara. Never seen this room looking so well."

17

Jenny liked it too. The walls were painted green with a narrow band of gold which, she guessed, must hide the tide-mark. Facing the window was a row of pictures from illustrated journals mounted in black frames. A mirror, framed in black and gold, hung above the mantelpiece which was draped in the same brown velvet as the curtains. Four brass candlesticks were ranged along it, two on either side of the handsome bronze clock, and a perforated brass fender guarded the hearth. A brass oil-lamp hung from the ceiling.

Jenny, looking at the heavy mahogany furniture thought that her aunt must need a great deal of help to move her furniture when the floods came.

"Never seen it look so well," said Mr Lovett again. "Even now, when the sun's round the back of the house, it looks warm and rich. It was always so gloomy."

"Yes," said Aunt Clara with quiet satisfaction. "I got it how I want it now. This is where I entertain my friends, the Waspes, on a Sunday evenin'. You don't know Amos and Harriet, Edward. They come to the town six year ago, an' took over Crosby's, the chemist's. You won't hear a finer preacher than Amos Waspe, nor meet a better couple of Christians than him an' Harriet."

A reflective smile softened her features. No one would ever guess the joy that filled her heart on Sunday evenings when she opened the parlour door for the Waspes and saw a beautiful room that was entirely her own creation. She had gutted it after her mother died, and used the insurance money to realize a dream she had had for years. It was the first pleasant dream of Clara Lovett's that had ever come true.

Jenny had walked into the middle of the room and was gazing at the little round table in the corner to the right of the fireplace. The large family Bible sat on top of it with a black-bordered photograph on each side. She knew that the elderly couple sitting stiffly, with a potted palm behind them, must be her grandparents, and that the sternly handsome fisherman leaning against a boat was Uncle Alfred. They stared back at her as though they knew she did not like them

18

and would never forgive them for the way they had treated her father and mother. Did they resent her being here? She shivered suddenly and was glad to run out of the room when her father called from the foot of the stairs.

Photographs of yachts and fishing-boats with their crews marched up the staircase wall, and as soon as Aunt Clara opened the door of the back bedroom Jenny's eye was caught by a large, framed text:

'They that go down to the sea in
ships, that do business in great waters;
These see the works of the Lord
and His wonders in the deep.'

You could not forget for a moment that this had been a fisherman's house, Jenny thought, even though the last fishermen to live in it had been dead for over seven years.

"This was yer father's room," Aunt Clara said. "Yer father's and Alfred's. And a wild, noisy pair they were too. I slep' beneath them in the kitchen. So I know."

There were bare floorboards, whitewashed walls, an old oak wardrobe that leaned a little to one side and a chipped marble wash-stand with a fly-spotted mirror above it. The high brass bed smelled of sheets that had blown dry in a salty, north-east wind. Jenny could imagine two boys thumping about in here, jumping on to the big bed and having pillow-fights. For a moment she felt a sharp longing for her old bedroom in Latimer Gardens with its pink carpet, rosebud wallpaper and muslin-draped dressing-table. Then she crossed to the open sash-window and looked out.

The air was strong with the tang of sea and marsh. The latter stretched out, right from the foot of the garden, it seemed, a spongy emerald carpet, criss-crossed by ditches, to the distant river, whose winding course was marked by white-sailed yachts. To the left, little wedges of blue sea showed in the gaps between buildings. The depression Jenny had felt on looking out at the marshes from the train changed to a kind of intoxication now. There was a private game she had played in London when riding on the tops of buses. She had imagined that she had spring-heeled boots and could leap along by the side of the bus over garden walls and fences. Here, already, her imagination had her soaring with the birds above the empty green plain.

Her father suddenly put a hand on her shoulder as though to steady her.

"You mustn't ever go wandering out there on your own, Jen," he said anxiously. "Local folks know the footpaths, but it's risky for strangers. There are holes out there that are bottomless."

"I'll look after the gel, Edward. I surely hope you can trust me to do that!" Aunt Clara sounded wounded.

She's touchy, thought Jenny in surprise, as she turned and saw her aunt's stitched-up mouth and pink cheeks. If she's not a dragon, I bet she can be a hedgehog at times.

Mr Lovett made soothing noises and they all went downstairs again. Aunt Clara could keep her news back no longer. She sat on her chair at the head of the table, hands folded in front of her.

"An old friend of yours come to the door last night, Edward," she started. "Bob Blowers from Lowestoft."

"Old Bob!" exclaimed Mr Lovett.

"Yes. He's skipper of the drifter *Good Hope* now. An' he were in a proper fix. His mate had apparently got hisself thirty days for bein' drunk an' disorderly. An' the *Good Hope*'s off to North Shields on Monday mornin'. Bob had been talkin' to Lucky Fulcher down on the quay and he'd mentioned you'd be home today. So Bob come to me to see if you'd be interested in a berth."

"And you said, 'Yes', Clara?"

"I did. I didn't like answerin' fer you. But I were afraid you'd lose the berth. And it is a start, though it is only fer three weeks. Did I do right?"

"Did you do right?" Mr Lovett's delighted laugh rang out as he began to make a neat pile of the garments that still lay on the dresser. "Clara, my girl, that's the best news I've heard in two months."

Jenny was still struggling out of the wave of apprehension that had broken over her at the thought of her father leaving on Monday, when Aunt Clara added, "An' I've good news for Jenny too. Lucky you told me she were smart an' had passed her Standard Six, Edward. I just mentioned to Mrs Gale one day she'd be lookin' for a job. An' she came up with this offer. The Gales' son, Josh (he's eleven), don't go back to school till next year. The curate tutor him mornin's. They don't like him playin' with the local lads. An' all their friends' children are away at school, so he wander about by hisself most afternoons, an' his mother think he need young company. Do you come with me an' help in the kitchen mornin's, Jenny, then play with young Josh afternoons, Mrs Gale will pay you four shillin' a week. What do you think to that?"

It was an embarrassing situation which Jenny did not know how to handle. Poor Aunt Clara obviously thought Jenny would be delighted by her good fortune. Working as a kitchen-maid! Imagine having to write and tell that piece of news to Mary or Miss Grant! She felt a giggle bubbling up inside and clamped her lips shut. Then she stared down at her boots and waited for her father to turn down Aunt Clara's well-meaning proposal in the tactful way that grown-ups have.

Instead, to her utter disbelief, she heard him say after a moment, "Yes, well, I'm sure Jenny will be happy to do that, Clara. Only you'll have to be patient with her. She's not used to domestic chores. Mrs Harris would never let her do anything around the house."

"Time she were learnin' then, Edward," said Aunt Clara firmly. "Good job she come here."

Jenny raised horrified eyes to her father. But he had turned his back and was standing staring down at his gear on the dresser, hands in his pockets, as though absorbed in his own reflections. It was the first time in her life that he had betrayed her. She felt as though the world were coming to an end.

Chapter 4

It was not the end of the world, of course. Nor even the end of Jenny's schooldays. It was just a matter of marking time, her father said, an interlude, until he had made enough money to take them back to London. Then he would find Jenny a private tutor to make up for the schooling she had lost, and enter her for an Upper School – perhaps even Woodside Girls Upper School where Mary Moore would be waiting for her.

But why couldn't she go to school in Newbrigg? Jenny demanded.

Because they were dependent on Clara's charity, was the answer. They had virtually nothing of their own left and if Aunt Clara had not taken them in they would have had to go on the parish. They could hardly ask Aunt Clara to keep Jenny at school, when she was obviously expected to work and contribute towards her keep.

I don't think it's that at all, Jenny wanted to protest. It just hasn't occurred to Aunt Clara that I might want to stay on at school. If you explained to her, I'm sure she'd agree to it. But, seeing the bleak look that had returned to her father's eyes, she held her tongue.

"It will only be for eleven months at most," he pointed out. "Like a long school holiday. It's as bad for me, you know, having to go back to sea."

Jenny felt a stab of guilt. Until then it had not crossed her mind that her father might find the life of a fisherman extremely rough after having been a shopkeeper for fourteen years. She took his arm and said firmly, "Well, if you can cope with it, I expect I can too. But I only hope they can put up with me at Galaxy House. The boy part will be all right. But I'm a duffer at housework."

"Clara will take you under her wing," her father assured her.

This conversation took place on Sunday morning, while Mr Lovett was showing Jenny around Newbrigg. Afterwards, whenever she came to a certain corner, or saw a particular shop, Jenny remembered what they had said there as clearly as if they had written their words on the footpath in indelible ink.

It was an ideal time to view the town – when the streets were empty of people and traffic – which was why Mr Lovett had taken the risk of offending his sister, who had assumed he and Jenny would go with her to chapel. At the foot of Wall Road, where the grimy-windowed Jolly Mariners pub squatted on the right-hand corner, with Jarvis's, the ships' chandler's facing it, they crossed over, past Jarvis's into the broad High Street. Mr Lovett pointed out the shops that Jenny would go to. "Working-folks' shops," he said. "They give tick to the fishermen's wives till their men come home."

Jenny, who had been looking forward eagerly to seeing the beach was, at first, bitterly disappointed when they reached the sea-front. There was not a grain of sand to be seen. Just a steep slope of stones at the foot of which the blue sea lazily sucked and lapped. Because it was the end of the season there was only one bathing-machine, obviously waiting to be hauled away for winter storage. And behind the fishing-boats, pulled up on the shingle, was a general litter of lobster-pots, fish-boxes and smelly heaps of fish refuse, over which flies and bluebottles buzzed. She could not imagine why people came here for their summer holiday when they might go to Broadstairs. Yet there must still be rich visitors in the hotels and boarding-houses, for there were liveried chauffeurs strolling along the promenade and pretty nursemaids pushing perambulators. "Just like my mother did," Jenny said to herself.

She was reminded of her mother again that afternoon, when her father took her along to the quay where the rescue of the toy lamb had taken place. Aunt Clara, in a mothball-scented, black Sunday dress, had earlier served up a dinner of cold beef and salad, before stacking the dirty dishes in the sink and retiring to the parlour to read her Bible. She had said very little during the meal, but her silence had been thoughtful, not sulky. The sermon that morning, she informed them, had been "very meaty".

When Jenny and her father arrived at the Jolly Mariners, they turned right into River Walk.

"Now you're going to see the real Newbrigg," Mr Lovett announced.

They walked past a row of flint-cobbled cottages where every door was open wide to the pavement. Dinner-time sounds floated out – the clatter of pots and cutlery, interspersed by snatches of talk. There was a strong smell of frying fish.

"They're not keeping the Sabbath Day holy! They're cooking," Jenny whispered.

"Some are too poor to be holy," her father said drily. "You can't cook fish and keep it overnight. And that's all they have to eat."

Facing the cottages, and stretching as far as the beach, was a wide green, where a few brown fishing-nets dangled limply between tall poles. At the far end was a long, two-storeyed brick building with doors on both levels. "The net factory," Mr Lovett told Jenny.

They passed Field's boat-building yard which smelled of wood-shavings and tar, then the ropeworks, and a large old pub called The Safe Return, standing on the corner of the quay.

The dilapidated-looking cottages on the opposite side of the road – some of them with shutters hanging askew and bald patches on their roofs – straggled on southwards beyond the quay towards a building of tarred weatherboarding with a wooden tower beside it.

"That's the Beach Company's shed along there. And the look-out tower," Mr Lovett said, coming to a halt and putting a hand on Jenny's shoulder.

"The Beach Company? Entertainers, do you mean? Comedians?" Jenny was thinking of the minstrels at Broadstairs.

24

Her father roared with laughter. "There were certainly a few comedians among them in my day. And I daresay there are some still. No, love," he went on, taking pity on her, "the Beach Company's a kind of association that has its own lifeboat. A different lifeboat from the Institute, although they help to man that, too. But the Company does salvage work as well as saving lives. If a ship's in trouble and the Company brings her in, the insurance people have to pay them. There was one year – 1885 it must have been – when your grandfather was cox'n of the Company boat, I was second cox'n and Alfred was bowman."

Jenny smiled up at him, stupidly shy all of a sudden. She had never dreamed that her father had been a lifeboat-man. Why hadn't he ever told her? She felt proud, naturally. But also a little uneasy. Up until yesterday her father had belonged only to herself and her dead mother. Now, it seemed, others were staking a claim on him. Those stern faces in the photographs in the parlour. Aunt Clara. The Beach Company.

"Hey, there! Ted!" Mr Lovett was hailed by one of a group of blue-jerseyed men standing further along the quay. Jenny watched him raise his hand in greeting and sensed that he wanted to join them but was reluctant to leave her.

"Go and talk to them, Dad. I can look around on my own," she said.

"Are you sure? It will only be for a few minutes. Some of those lads I haven't seen for years, you see."

"Of course! I'm not a baby."

Still, when Jenny suddenly remembered that, the next morning, her father would be leaving her not for a few minutes, but for three weeks, she did not feel quite so grown up and confident. In fact, she began to wish with all her heart that they had brought Mrs Harris to Newbrigg with them. She could have slept with me in that great, cold bed, she thought, and kept house for Aunt Clara. But thinking of Mrs Harris set her eyes pricking alarmingly and she had to set off determinedly down the quay, taking her straw hat off and swinging it by its elastic, so that at least she would look

25

carefree. Imagining how she looked to other people always helped Jenny if she were struggling against tears. She was soon able to stop swallowing hard and blinking and to have a proper look at the various buildings that seemed to have been thrown down, higgledy-piggledy along one side of the quay.

There were several red brick warehouses with large, faded letters on their sides. She could make out SALT on one and COAL on another. And between these fairly large buildings were little rows of black sheds, each with a name painted on its door. She recognized 'Block' and 'Fulcher'. But there were other very unusual names: 'Greathead', 'Flowerdew', 'Half-night'.

Some of the sheds had their doors lying open and from the ropes, oars, fishing-rods and other paraphernalia stacked inside came a mingled smell of sea-water, tar and fresh paint. Jenny crossed to the edge of the quay and looked down to see several gently rocking rowing-boats moored to rings in the wall. In mid-channel there were yachts riding at anchor and what she guessed were a couple of fishing-smacks. From somewhere on the marshes a bird was calling with a liquid trilling note and a moment later she heard laughter from the group of fishermen behind her.

Jenny suddenly felt tired. "The sea air," she told herself. She walked over to a bollard, sat down and closed her eyes for a few minutes. When she opened them she found her father standing a few feet away from her with such a peculiar expression on his face that she immediately jumped up and ran over to him.

"Dad! Are you all right?" she cried.

"Yes. I'm all right, Jen," he said slowly. "I just hadn't realized how like your mother you were growing. In that green dress . . ."

"It's turquoise."

"Is it? Well, anyway, you do look very like her today. The lads were saying so, too."

"Thank you," said Jenny after a moment. She knew that her father had paid her a great compliment, for he had worshipped her mother.

Mr Lovett said as much to Aunt Clara next morning, when he was taking leave of them at the gate at six o'clock. He hoisted his seaman's bag on to his shoulder in preparation for the long walk to the station and drew Jenny tightly to his side, slipping a silver shilling into her hand.

"Take care of this one for me, Clara," he said. "I lost half my world ten years ago. This is all that's left to me. All that really matters, I mean."

Aunt Clara was standing on the other side of the white wooden gate, so that Jenny was sure she was not imagining the change that came over her aunt when her father made this little speech. For the past hour Jenny and Aunt Clara had been working together in womanly determination to see that Mr Lovett would have every possible comfort they could shove in his duffle-bag to soften the hardships of his first trip, and had given him a good breakfast of porridge, eggs and bacon to start him off. They had been chatting a little – even exchanging an occasional joke – but now, as Aunt Clara looked from Mr Lovett to Jenny, both her face and her voice lost their warmth.

"Of course I'll look after the child," she said curtly. "I owe it to you, Edward. After all, I am a-sittin' in your house."

"*Your* house," said Mr Lovett emphatically. "You earned it. You know that, Clara." Jenny thought he sounded almost angry.

Then he kissed Jenny on the forehead, patted Aunt Clara on the shoulder and strode off up the hill, to disappear round the bend without having once looked back.

It's because he couldn't bear to, thought Jenny, hot tears rolling down her cheeks.

"Come along," called Aunt Clara, turning away. "You can help me tie up the washing. Mrs Nightingale from River Walk come up to wash fer the Gales Monday mornin's, an' she do mine along with theirs." There was no trace of sympathy in her tone.

Jenny followed her indoors, dashing away her tears. She found herself longing for Mrs Harris's warm, cushiony bosom and the funny Scots sayings she would have produced, with an accompanying peppermint, to cheer Jenny up. But Mrs Harris was hundreds of miles away. So were Mary and Miss Grant. And by this evening Dad would be too. She only had Aunt Clara. "So you'd better make the best of it," she told herself firmly, and ran upstairs to fetch the dirty towels from the wash-stands to put in with the rest of the washing.

Chapter 5

To keep her spirits up, Jenny had put on her turquoise Sunday dress and her newest white pinafore for her first day at work.

"Now, soon as we git there you'll start cuttin' the bread for the master's an' mistress's mornin' tea," Aunt Clara began as they left Mariners Terrace at quarter-past seven to walk up to Galaxy House. "An' see you cut it thin enough! After that you can cut Master Josh's bread what he eat after his porridge. He like that a bit thicker. You'll have yer breakfast with Catchpole an' me an' Jeremiah Double, the handyman. Then you'll help Catchpole lay the table in the dinin'-room. Catchpole's the housemaid, by the way. You can help me in the kitchen till the master leave for the station. Then Mrs Gale want to have a look at you in the mornin'-room. After that . . ."

Jenny stopped listening. What was the point? Aunt Clara would let her know soon enough what she had to do when the time came. It was bad enough having had to watch Dad walk off in that stiff, determined way as though he were hurting all over, without being reminded that she was a servant-girl now. What would Mrs Harris say if she knew? Or Miss Grant? Feeling a lump rise ominously in her throat, she determinedly forced her thoughts in another direction. Aunt Clara's manner was still noticeably cool. Something had upset her badly that morning when Dad was saying good-bye to them. Could it have been that remark about Jenny being all that he had left?

She had wondered about that at the time, feeling that it wasn't very tactful with Aunt Clara standing there.

Now she cast a sidelong look at her aunt and noticed for the first time the two little curling black hairs sprouting from her chin. How dowdy she looked, too, in her black coat, carrying her pillowcase of washing. Jenny thought it pretty certain that Aunt Clara would die an old maid. Aunt Clara doubtless thought so too. And now she had lost all of her family except Dad and Jenny. Poor woman! Jenny wracked her brains for something to say to her that would make up for Mr Lovett's tactlessness.

Before inspiration came, however, they had turned into the wide rutted track that led to the side entrance of Galaxy House. There were double iron gates for wheeled vehicles and a narrow wooden door, with a high lintel set into the wall. Jenny followed her aunt through the door into a walled courtyard with a stable block and several outhouses. A chest-nut tree was shedding green-jacketed conkers over the cobbles.

"That tree was nuthin' like that size when I first come here," Aunt Clara observed as they walked towards the house. "Miss Margot, the eldest daughter, were jest one year old, an' her nanny used to lay her in her perambulator under that tree so's she could watch the leaves. An' now she's married an' soon to have a babe of her own. An' Miss Freda married too. Can't hardly believe it!"

"How many are there in the family?" asked Jenny.

"Jest the three. Miss Margot, Miss Freda an' Master Josh."

So Josh really is a tail-ender, Jenny thought. He must feel just like an only child.

"Doesn't the boy collect the conkers?" she asked, re-membering the fights amongst the boys at home for the shiny brown nuts that dropped from the big chestnut trees border-ing the local park.

"Master Josh?" said Aunt Clara with a short laugh. "He think of nuthin' but birds. Birds on the brain he has. His father despair of him."

Jenny recalled the cowed-looking boy she had seen with his angry father on Saturday afternoon and, before she realized it, found herself taking his part.

"I don't see what's wrong with being keen on birds. I like birds, don't you, Aunt Clara?"

Her aunt, who had had her hand on the latch of the back door, wheeled round at this as though Jenny had struck her. She looked furious. "No! I don't like birds as it happen," she snapped. "I hates them."

Jenny was dumbfounded – and embarrassed. Why should anyone hate birds? she wondered as she followed Aunt Clara into a small dark lobby lined with boots, long brushes and buckets. But she had no time to worry about her aunt's eccentricities now. She must watch where they were going and learn the lay-out of the house as quickly as possible, she decided.

The lobby led into a small rectangular hall. To the right was the green baize door that led to the front part of the house. Aunt Clara hung up her coat and hat on a hook on the wall as somewhere a clock struck the half-hour.

"Come along now," she said sharply to Jenny, and hurried ahead of her into the kitchen.

I bet she's never been late for work once in twenty-one years, Jenny thought.

The kitchen was large but gloomy because of its dismal colour scheme. There was chocolate-coloured oilcloth on the floor, dark brown cupboards and dressers and bottle-green walls. A big kettle hissed on top of the central boiler of a massive black range. Everything looked larger than life to Jenny.

Aunt Clara took a loaf of bread from a wooden bin and a long knife from a drawer and set them at the end of the table. "Get you started then!" she ordered.

Jenny was so nervous that, to begin with, the knife jiggled up and down in her shaking hand, almost out of control. She never had been much of an expert at bread-cutting, mainly because she had not had much practice. But, finally, with a great effort of will and a painfully tight grip on the knife's ivory handle, she managed to produce four neat, thin slices.

"Can't you work no faster than that, gel?" Aunt Clara called irritably from the range where she was filling cans with hot water for the wash-stands upstairs.

Jenny's cheeks burned. She was not used to criticism, either at home or at school. She hurriedly cut another slice of bread, wafer-thin, and it disintegrated before it hit the breadboard. From then on her morning went from bad to worse. Catchpole, the housemaid, turned out to be a stout, childish young woman with an uncertain temper. When she came morosely into the kitchen at eight o'clock she had been at work for two hours. She had lit six fires, including the kitchen-range, and swept and dusted five rooms. So she was not inclined to smile forgivingly when Jenny spilled milk on the carpet as she carried a laden tray through the green door, or when she allowed a greasy slice of bacon to slide on to the white cloth as she gazed admiringly round the dining-room at the decorated frieze, the marble fireplace and the green velvet curtains. Indeed, whenever Aunt Clara was out of earshot, Catchpole was downright unpleasant.

"Little Dead-Slow-an'-Stop!" she whispered vindictively, and once gave Jenny a spiteful pinch on the arm as she passed her in the passage.

Jenny stood in corners watching numbly while her aunt cooked three different dishes at once and Catchpole scurried to and fro between the kitchen and the dining-room. Set to washing the dishes, she took so long to scrub the egg-stains from the first one that Catchpole pushed her impatiently out of the way and did the job herself. When asked by Jeremiah Double, the wrinkled little gardener-handyman, to carry a vase of gladioli through to the morning-room before Mrs Gale went in, she took them to the drawing-room by mistake.

At twenty-five past ten Jenny was conducted to the morning-room by Aunt Clara, to be scrutinized by the mistress of the house. Mrs Gale was a handsome woman with a very firm, straight mouth, a high forehead and auburn hair brushed back to make a halo round her face. She raised her eyes from the letter she was reading, stared rather absently at Jenny for a minute, then smiled faintly and nodded her approval.

"Well, she seem to think you look all right anyway," Aunt Clara whispered with a sigh of relief, pushing Jenny out of the door, whilst she stayed behind to discuss the day's menus with her mistress.

As Jenny walked back across the front hall with its dark oak tables and settles and dingy oil-paintings of ships and stormy seas, the grandfather clock at the foot of the stairs struck a single funereal note. Unhappiness swelled inside her chest like a balloon, threatening to suffocate her. To think of all the hours and days and weeks she would have to spend here! Eleven months her father had said. They stretched ahead like some bleak Arctic waste. How was she going to survive them?

Catchpole, Jeremiah Double and Mrs Nightingale, the washerwoman, were in the kitchen having their morning tea-break when Jenny walked in. She knew by the way they fell instantly silent that they they had been talking about her, or perhaps about Aunt Clara. Catchpole made a show of being friendly and pouring out a cup of tea for Jenny. But she dropped this pretence as soon as Mr Double had returned to his digging and Mrs Nightingale to her bubbling copper. When she had set a tray with a cup of tea, a glass of milk and a plate of biscuits, she thrust it at Jenny.

"Here," she said sourly, "see if you can't do suthin' right for a change. Go up the back stair – through that door in the corner over there. Schoolroom's on the first landin'. Give this to Master Josh an' the curate."

Jenny opened the door, holding the heavy tray one-handed, while Catchpole stood smirking. Then she began to stumble up a dark, narrow staircase where all the unpleasant cooking smells seemed to have fled and lingered. Halfway up she caught her right elbow on the wall and a wave of tea slopped into the saucer. It was almost the last straw. A sob rose in her throat. Now she understood why children who were duffers at school sat low down in their seats, shrinking into themselves. Other people's scorn could eat you away. She felt truly sorry for all the times she had joined in unkind laughter at people who mispronounced words or made frightful spelling mistakes.

She reached the landing, then paused as she was about to knock on the schoolroom door. Josh was having a French lesson and obviously struggling with his irregular verbs.

"What is the point of my giving you work to do on your own, boy, if you consistently fail to do it?" Mr Hanley was demanding crossly in a pronounced Welsh accent.

Jenny thought that a curate ought to be more forbearing. Poor Josh! This was the second time she had overheard him being told off. She knocked loudly, then pushed the door open, cutting short the boy's scolding. Mr Hanley, a thin, sandy-haired young man, sat at a large table-desk with his back to the tall sash-windows, while Josh, at a smaller desk nearer the centre of the room, faced his tutor. The curate barely glanced at Jenny as he took the tray from her, but Josh stared at her curiously, making Jenny's face burn with mortification because she felt like his servant. As she left, she caught sight of the maps and the blackboard on the walls on either side of the fireplace. She found herself aching to be back in Laurel Park School again with Mary and her other friends. She loved lessons. She didn't mind working at French verbs. Why should she be waiting on some stupid little boy? It wasn't fair! Dad should never have agreed to it.

But thinking of her father was almost Jenny's undoing. For several minutes as she stood on the dark landing, she teetered on the verge of breaking down completely. It was with a great effort that she finally pulled herself together and hurried back down to the kitchen where Aunt Clara immediately set her to work, preparing the vegetables for lunch. She did this as badly as she had done everything else that morning, paring great lumps off the potatoes and carrots along with their skins and leaving tough strings on the runner beans.

"You are some stoopid fer a great gel!" cried Catchpole

when she saw the beans. And Aunt Clara showed that she agreed with her by maintaining a tight-lipped silence.

"If I make you feel as bad as that, you had better tell your mother and I'll go back downstairs." Jenny stood scowling at the books in the bureau-bookcase between the two school-room windows. Aunt Clara had given her her dinner with Josh in the kitchen at half-past twelve, then had sent them both upstairs. They had been in the schoolroom now for a full ten minutes and, in all the time since dinner, Josh had not said a single word to her. What was worse, since they had come into the schoolroom, he had begun to sigh loudly, sitting at his desk with his chin sunk on his chest.

"I'm not depressed about you," he said now, waving his hand in the irritable way of someone who has great problems on his mind and is being pestered by a gnat. "It's Mr Hanley. He says if I don't show any improvement by the end of the week, he'll tell my father that there's no point in his coming any more. And you know what that will mean!"

"A thrashing?"

"Not necessarily. But definitely school," Josh said gloomily.

"Lucky you!"

"What?"

"Never mind." Jenny was determined not to set foot on the treacherous slide of self-pity again. "What's the trouble? The French verbs?"

"Oh, you heard, did you? Yes. Those. And the Latin. And the English. And the history."

"Probably all you need is someone to listen to you."

Jenny sat down at Mr Hanley's desk and looked at Josh appraisingly. He was the kind of small, skinny, big-eyed boy that girls have a compulsion to mother. She began to feel less unhappy as she considered how she could help him.

"I'll listen to you, if you like," she went on. "We could start with the French verbs. My friend, Mary Moore, and I helped each other with those last term. Miss Grant said it was the best way to learn them. You can do it anywhere, if one person has the book. Walking along the road. Sitting on a bus."

Josh looked towards the window. Through the green cloud of the chestnut tree the sky was blue.

"What about in a boat?" he asked. "I must go up the river today. I want to look for a bird."

Jenny hesitated. She had never been in a boat in her life, not even at Broadstairs – Mrs Harris had been too nervous. She could swim two lengths of the school baths, though. And her father had not said she must not go on the river. He had warned her against the marshes, but not the river. To be on the safe side, should she ask Aunt Clara? Then she remembered that Mrs Gale was entertaining a guest to lunch and Aunt Clara would be very busy. Besides, she thought, if Josh were allowed to go out in boats on his own, he must know what he was doing.

"Yes," she said finally. "I don't see why not."

"Good." Josh brightened up immediately. He grinned at her, then suddenly jumped to his feet and slid across the shiny oilcloth floor to a door in the corner beyond the window. "Come in if you like," he called.

She walked over to poke her head round the door and look into Josh's small, shabby, crowded bedroom, with its faded green paper peeling from the walls and very old, scratched furniture. There was an iron wash-stand, of a type she had never seen before, shaped like a church font and narrow enough to fit into the corner beside the courtyard window. Before the opposite window, which looked out towards the sea, there was a telescope on a brass stand.

Josh had almost disappeared inside the big mahogany ward-robe which stood alongside his bed. When he emerged he was brandishing a pair of binoculars, which he hung round his neck.

"Can't do without these," he said. "They're my most treasured possession."

He squeezed past her and ran over to the bureau-bookcase in

35

the schoolroom, where he picked out a French grammar book, and handed it to Jenny.

"Do you see all those spaces?" He pointed to gaps of varying widths on the four shelves. "Those were my ornithology books. Father took them all away on Saturday in his towering rage. He's probably burned them by now. And if you want to know why, it was because I lost my race through suddenly seeing this marvellous rare bird called a roller. Then, of course, I made things worse by telling him I was definitely going to be an ornithologist and not run his rotten old brewery . . . It's the roller I'm going to look for today – in the unlikely event it hasn't been shot yet."

"Shot? Why would anyone shoot it? Is it like a pheasant?" Jenny had seen pheasants hanging in poultry shops in London and had always felt sorry, because, even when dead, they looked beautiful.

"If you mean can you eat it, the answer's 'no'. Whoever shoots it will sell it to a taxidermist. A bird-stuffer. Then its poor corpse will sit mouldering in some museum, or, even worse, in a private house, where people can't even see how beautiful it was." Josh's voice was tight with disapproval.

"Do you mean that all those birds I saw in the Natural History Museum were killed?"

"What did you think? That they'd died of scarlet fever?"

"No . . . I don't know . . . that they had just died . . . of natural causes." Jenny was really shaken by this lurid revelation. All the enjoyment of her excursions with Miss Grant faded.

Josh looked at her narrowly to see if she were teasing. When he was sure she was in earnest he said warmly, "I'm glad you feel the same way as I do. No one else here does. Well, almost no one."

Jenny remembered how her aunt had shocked her that morning.

"Yes," she said. "Even Aunt Clara, who's so religious, told me that she hated birds."

Josh's eyes widened. "I shouldn't talk about birds to Miss Lovett," he said quickly.

"Why not?"

"You don't want to upset her. After all, you have to live with her."

"But why should . . ."

"Come on!" Josh cut her short by opening the door into the carpeted corridor that led to the front of the house. "We'll go out this way. You can start asking me the verbs."

"They've left Grandfather's room exactly as it was when he died three years ago," he told Jenny in a low voice. "I'll show it to you one day."

Jenny did not know that she wanted to see the room. It sounded rather eerie. But she kept her reservations to herself. As they went down the front stairs she heard Josh go through the present tense of *être*. She made him say it three more times before they reached the front door.

"You see!" she said triumphantly. "Word perfect already!"

Neither of them noticed that Mrs Gale had slipped out of the dining-room and was looking thoughtfully after them.

Every grown-up they met between Galaxy House and the quay gave Josh some sort of greeting. The doctor sounded the horn of his motor, which was chugging up the hill in a cloud of dust. A couple of fishermen nodded their heads. A sailor touched his yachting-cap. Old Mrs Fulcher, standing in her doorway, called, "Good day, Master Josh," in her crackling voice. When a thick-set fisherman with black, curling hair and earrings grinned at Jenny too, Josh told her he was her next-door neighbour, Bulldog Block.

"Why is he called Bulldog?" Jenny turned to look after the man. "He's quite handsome."

"He was bitten by one. On an unmentionable part of his anatomy." Josh watched Jenny slyly out of the corner of his eyes. "Bet you're wondering where!"

To her annoyance she felt her face grow hot. "And what

about Lucky Fulcher?" she asked stiffly. "I suppose he was bitten on a mentionable part. That's why he's lucky."

Josh grinned. "Good guess," he said. "But actually it's because he's so superstitious. Most of the fishermen are, of course. But Fulcher beats the band. Grandfather had terrible trouble with him at one time. He would refuse to sail if he met a parson on his way to the quay. Or if anyone on his boat said the word 'rabbit'. He still won't go to sea on a Friday. And if a woman so much as breathes on his boat he has hysterics. Personally I think he takes after his old mother. She's a witch if ever I met one."

As they walked up the quay Josh said, "We'd better leave the verbs until we're on the water. If you're not used to boats, I'll have to tell you what to do."

They skirted a group of men reading a sale notice pinned to the door of a shed.

"Over here," said Josh, leading Jenny to the edge of the quay.

She looked over and saw an iron ladder with green, slimy-looking rungs. At its foot a rowing-boat was moored.

"Just watch how I get into it," Josh told her, "and do exactly the same. Take your time. There's no hurry."

Five minutes later she was sitting in the middle of the boat, on what Josh called the thwart, watching his lean brown arms energetically wielding the oars as he rowed them upriver. There were a few yachts moored in mid-channel and many more with their bows almost touching the high grassy banks. Josh told her that the owners of these had left them there for the winter.

"And, by the way, you call it the wall. Not the bank. The river-wall. We could have walked along it to reach the punt. But it's quicker by water . . . I'm ready for more verbs now, please."

He had learned *aller, avoir* and *connaître* by the time they reached the ramshackle little jetty, to which was moored a very long, shallow, grey boat, decked over at each of its pointed ends and with a square open well in the middle. The name *Moondrop* was painted on its side.

"After one of Grandfather's cutters," said Josh, as he made the painter of the rowing-boat fast, then helped Jenny to climb out. "It's fairly ancient, but it's the ideal craft for bird-watching. It's so low that I can easily hide in the reeds. And it has only a few inches draught, which means I can go up the shallowest creeks. If I want to get really close to the birds I lie flat on my stomach and use the short paddles."

Having seen that Jenny was safely settled in the punt, he cast off. The boat shot forward as the light oars cut through the water. Jenny no longer felt motherly towards Josh. Now he was the competent one and she the ignoramus.

"What can I do?" she enquired meekly.

"Just sing out whenever you see any birds. We'll go upriver as far as Decoy Point."

"What does the roller look like?" she asked.

As soon as Josh described the bird, Jenny remembered the parrot she had thought she had seen from the train.

"Yes. That would be it," Josh said, when she had told him about it. "It could have gone further inland. But it may still be around. So keep your eyes skinned."

Jenny relaxed. It was very soothing to be floating along just inches above the water. Like a swan, she thought dreamily. The sun penetrated the thin fabric of her dress, cocooning her in a comforting warmth. Above, white puffballs of cloud inched their way across the blue sky.

"Do you come here every day?" she asked Josh. He had stopped rowing and was sweeping the sky with his binoculars, allowing the boat to drift with the tide.

"No. I go to the North Marsh a lot, especially in the nesting season. It's marvellous there for redshanks and lapwings. And I go along the beach when the migrant birds are coming in from the sea. I come here mostly on mercy missions."

"Mercy missions?"

Josh dropped his binoculars and started rowing again. Jenny stared at him. It was as though, inside the boy, a light had dimmed.

"I call them that," he said in a flat voice. "I come after they've been shooting. To look for the wounded birds. They creep away into the reeds and up on the wall, you see. If I don't find them, they either die slowly in agony, or the rats get them."

Jenny sat up straight, gripping the sides of the punt. "But what do you do with them?"

"Most of them are too far gone to be helped. I have to wring their necks," he said shortly. Then he added, "But we always manage to save a few."

"Oh, Josh! How can you?" It was the idea of Josh's having to kill what he loved that made Jenny cry out and screw up her face. Having to kill over and over again. With his bare hands.

"Someone has to do it."

"What did you mean when you said, 'we'. You said, 'We always manage to save some.' "

"Did I? I didn't mean to. It was a slip of the tongue." Josh was now looking over his shoulder as he rowed, his face turned away from her.

They spent two hours on the water, exploring both the creeks that criss-crossed the saltings (the green marshy waste between the river and the wall) and the secret, whispering channels in the reed-beds. It was a novel world for Jenny, full of unexpected sights and sounds: a heron, hunchbacked, fishing in the shallows with his long, stabbing beak; a flock of widgeon circling, then landing on the water with an explosive "whoosh!"; little bunches of curlews making the melancholy bubbling calls that she had heard yesterday when sitting on the quay; swallows gathering on the wall, where goldfinches were busy about the thistle seeds.

Once, seeing a splash of orange and blue in the reeds, Jenny thought they had found the roller. But it turned out to be only a bearded tit.

By the time the rowing-boat was made fast to the quay again, it was four o'clock by Josh's watch and the tide was on the turn. Aunt Clara had told Jenny she must be back at Mariners Terrace for five o'clock tea.

"What are we going to do now?" she asked Josh as they walked away from the river.

"Well . . . actually . . ." Josh looked up at her anxiously.

"Yes?"

"I have some private business to attend to . . . if you don't mind, Jenny."

"Why should I mind?" In fact she was hurt and angry, and did not care if he saw it.

But Josh said, "Good!" quite happily, obviously choosing to believe Jenny's words rather than her face. "Some girls would have turned huffy when I said that. But I knew you were different. See you tomorrow, then," he finished cheerfully.

With a wave he ran off towards the Beach Company's shed, leaving Jenny standing outside The Safe Return. Where was he going in such a hurry? she wondered. As she watched, she saw him turn off the track just beyond the look-out tower and go down on to the marshes. He was probably still looking for his precious roller, she decided. Perhaps he thought she would be a hindrance to him on the marshes.

Jenny's resentment soon faded. Josh was an odd little boy. But she had enjoyed her afternoon with him. With his company to look forward to she might just survive all the mornings of humiliating drudgery. She decided to while away the hour before tea by going down to the beach. As she started to cross the drying-green, where lines of washing now hung among the fishing-nets, she suddenly remembered how she had walked here yesterday with her father. Was it really only yesterday? She felt as though it were weeks ago. What was Dad doing at this moment? she wondered. He had told her he might be seasick, it was so long since his last trip.

So absorbed was Jenny in her thoughts that she was scrunching along the shingle before she noticed the activity on the beach ahead of her. Several tan-sailed fishing-boats were coming in on the beginning of the ebb-tide, each with an attendant cloud of screaming gulls. Men, and a few boys, stood along the water's edge holding long, narrow boards. As each

41

boat hit the shingle, two boards were dropped in front of it. Then the end of a rope was attached to its keel and the men working the winch at the head of the beach began turning for all they were worth, hauling the boat up the steep slope.

Jenny scrambled hastily up on to the promenade to watch from a safe distance as more boats came in and the catches were rinsed and gutted on the beach. Then, hearing shouts, she looked up to see a gang of about a dozen wild-looking youngsters running along from the direction of the green. She did not wait to see if they were friendly, but quickly turned into Neptune Row, one of the cobbled alleyways that led off the promenade. She ran along it to the High Street.

Facing her was Maggs' sweet shop, the blinds of which had been drawn yesterday when she had passed it with her father. Now she ran across to have a leisurely look in the window and decide what she might buy with her shilling in the weeks ahead.

"Amos!" The woman's high voice carried clearly across the quiet street.

Jenny swung round to find that she was being watched by a thin, pale woman in a black dress, standing in the doorway of the chemist's shop. A bald man with spectacles and a bushy moustache came out to join her, and they both stared at Jenny until she flushed and wriggled with self-consciousness.

Indignantly, she abandoned the sweets and scurried off with lowered eyes towards Wall Road. Really, she thought, you would think that grown-ups would have better manners. It was only when she was passing the chandler's a few minutes later, that it suddenly dawned on her why the couple had found her so interesting. Of course! The chemist was Mr Waspe who preached at the chapel. And the woman must have been his wife. They were Aunt Clara's friends, who came round on Sunday evenings. They had probably just been wondering if she was Aunt Clara's niece.

I hope I didn't look rude, she thought anxiously, as she turned into Wall Road. I don't want to upset Aunt Clara. For she did seem rather easily upset. She mustn't be asked about her young days. And Josh said Jenny mustn't talk to her about birds. She paused, with her hand on the latch of the gate. The Blocks' front door was standing open and she could smell frying fish and hear children shouting and laughing. It all sounds so homely and normal, Jenny thought enviously, as she walked reluctantly up her aunt's path.

Chapter 6

At half-past eight that evening Jenny sat at the kitchen table chewing the end of her pencil. She had lit the oil-lamp and now pulled it forward, so that its light fell on the map of England and Wales in her atlas. She was trying to work out where her father's boat might be. It was her way of staving off the feeling of homesickness and loneliness that had been making her miserable since tea-time. Aunt Clara had made no comment about Jenny's poor performance that morning, but her stitched-up mouth and dark looks had spoken for themselves. In fact, it had been a relief when she had gone off to Galaxy House at six o'clock, leaving Jenny with only the ticking of the clock and the plop of an occasional falling cinder to break the silence in the kitchen. The frequent bursts of shouting and laughter that had been coming from the Blocks' garden up until an hour ago had only intensified her feeling of loneliness. She sighed and made a cross on the blue area beside Skegness. She did not really know if the *Good Hope* were anywhere near there. But she would pretend that it was.

The slamming of the front door made her jump and drop her pencil. Aunt Clara was back. Jenny panicked, almost opting for bed there and then rather than suffer an hour of her aunt's curt remarks and sullen silences. But Aunt Clara walked into the kitchen in a totally different mood from the one in which she had left it. There were two bright patches of colour on her cheeks and her eyes looked as though they had been polished.

"Well! Have I got news for *you*, gel!" she started, snatching her hat off, and sitting down opposite Jenny. "You're some clever mawther from what Mrs Gale say. Larnin' Master Josh his French! Reckon you never knew she were a-listenin' when you come down the stair this afternoon. She were, though! An' do you know what? She want you to have lessons mornin's with Master Josh 'stead of helpin' in the kitchen. She think that'll be competition for him, an' do him good. You should've seen that Catchpole's face when I told her. Whool-ly flabbergasted she were!" Aunt Clara gave an exultant little laugh and added fiercely, "Callin' my niece stoopid! I won't be forgettin' that in a hurry!"

Jenny hardly dared believe her good fortune.

"But what about the four shillings, Aunt Clara?" she asked breathlessly. "Mrs Gale won't pay me if I'm not working."

"She would've done," said Aunt Clara proudly. "But I said we wouldn't take it. Who care about four shillin'! " She pulled her hat on again. "Come along, Jenny," she ordered, "time you was a-meetin' the neighbours. Hurry now! We don't need no light. We're only goin' to Granny Fulcher an' the Blocks."

Jenny hurried out after her aunt into the cool night, thinking that it was rather late to be paying visits. Sure enough, they found old Mrs Fulcher's house in darkness and there was no answer to Aunt Clara's peremptory knock.

"No wonder she complain she can't sleep nights," Aunt Clara said crossly. "She go to bed far too early. You'd think she were a baby 'stead of an owd woman!"

She took Jenny's arm and hustled her round to the Blocks, as though she were afraid they, too, might all decide to go to bed before she caught them. In fact, as Jenny saw, when she followed Mr Block and her aunt into their neighbours' kitchen, the three youngest children were already in their nightclothes.

The Blocks' house was identical to Aunt Clara's in lay-out. But it had a totally different character. Jenny realized this as soon as she walked in the front door and sniffed the pungent smells of fish and sea and tar. It was almost like being down on the quay, or on the beach. Tarred rope lay coiled on the floor of the passage. They had to squeeze past a stack of empty fish-baskets. And black oilskins, dangling from hooks on the wall, stretched out stiff arms sequinned with fish scales.

In the kitchen, too, there was plenty of evidence of Mr Block's occupation. Several pairs of sea boots stood underneath the long table, at which a girl and two boys were sitting. Navy smocks and jerseys hung drying on a line above the range. The dresser was covered from end to end with fishing-lines, rope ends, nails, enormous needles and thimbles and various other objects which were unfamiliar to Jenny but which she realized must come from a boat. There were lines of photographs of boats and fishermen on the whitewashed walls, and, above the mantelpiece, a row of framed certificates which Mr Block had won for lifesaving.

"Well! If it ain't young Jenny Lovett! We've bin a-wonderin' when we was goin' to meet you, my mawther. Thought you was never goin' to bring her round, Clara." Mrs Block, young-looking in the lamplight, with dark hair falling softly across her forehead, had light, humorous eyes and a generous mouth. She was feeding a plump baby girl with bread and milk. An older girl and a little boy stood by her knee.

Mr Block had obviously been sitting in the fireside-chair opposite his wife, unravelling a tangle of fishing-lines which were spilling out of a basket on to the floor. Now he clapped a hand on Jenny's shoulder.

"Well? See what I mean? Who does this gel look like, Liza?" he asked his wife.

Mrs Block raised her head and stared at him.

"Why, I don't fare to know who the child look like, I'm sure," she said deliberately. "Like herself, I reckon. Do you see any likeness, Bulldog?"

"No . . . No . . . I reckon not." With an embarrassed laugh Mr Block sat down and started to work on his lines again.

45

Aunt Clara sat down too, on the other side of the table from the three young Blocks. She seemed very much at home.

"Lost their tongues, Liza, your young 'uns?" she asked jokingly. "That make some change."

"That do indeed, Clara," agreed Mrs Block with a smile.

The children at her knee, both in nightgowns, pressed close against her. The two boys at the table, who were whittling pieces of wood, giggled and nudged each other, while the sallow-faced girl did not look up from the sock she was darning, but turned bright pink.

"Reckon I'd better introduce them, Jenny," said Mrs Block after a moment. "That's Leila at the table, lookin' so shy. She's fourteen an' work in the baker's. Then there's Charlie an' Robert sittin' beside her. Charlie's twelve an' Robert's just ten. These two here a-tryin' to creep into my skirts are Lizbeth (she's eight) an' Samuel (he's six). An' this little owd cherub is baby Lucy."

The three at the table finally raised their heads to give Jenny embarrassed smiles, which she eagerly returned. As far as she was concerned the more friends she made the better, especially when she would not have any schoolmates. She was wondering whether she ought to go and sit beside them (nobody seemed to stand on ceremony in this household) when Aunt Clara said loudly, "Reason we come round, Liza, was to tell you what a bright gel this niece o' mine is. She's some clever! Can speak French an' everything. Matter o' fac', Mrs Gale want her to help the curate larn Master Josh his lessons every day. What do you think to that?"

Jenny could see immediately what Leila, Charlie and Robert thought. Their faces straightened and became wary. Their stares were no longer interested, but coldly curious. As though I were some sort of freak, Jenny thought in dismay. She tried hastily to repair the damage her aunt had done.

"Well, I'm not actually going to help the curate," she explained. "I'm not nearly clever enough to do that. I'm just going to have lessons with Josh, to keep him company."

Aunt Clara drew her breath in sharply and swung round to glare at Jenny.

"You callin' me a liar?" she demanded harshly. "You contradictin' me, gel? You sayin' Mrs Gale don't want you to help Master Josh with his lessons?"

Jenny was horrified. She backed against the dresser, her face scarlet, and knocked a pair of scissors on to the floor. She had always been taught that only rough, uncouth people raised their voices in public and made scenes. And here was Aunt Clara doing just that – and in someone else's house. What must the Blocks think of her? Surprisingly, not one of them looked particularly perturbed.

"The child's jest bein' modest, Clara," Mrs Block said calmly. She was rocking the baby, who had fallen asleep on her lap. "She take after Ted. He were always a shy, modest lad."

"Maybe," said Aunt Clara querulously. "But I don't like bein' made to look a liar."

As she turned again to scowl at Jenny, Mr Block suddenly dropped his fishing-lines and smacked his thigh.

"Blast!" he cried. "I almost forgot. I got a guernsey I want you to look at, Clara Lovett. That got a bloomin' great hole in it. Tore it on a hook. Liza don't think she can mend it."

"Where is it? Let me see it." Aunt Clara was already on her feet and looking around her at the various navy garments hanging over the backs of chairs.

"That's in the front room, Clara. Come and see."

As soon as Mr Block had led Aunt Clara out, his wife beckoned to Jenny to come over and sit on his chair.

"You gittin' along all right with yer aunt, my dear?" she whispered, leaning forward with a look of concern on her face.

Jenny nodded a shade uncertainly.

"Well, do you have any problems, come round to me," she went on quickly, all the time keeping an eye on the open door. "Even if you jest want a chat, I'll allus be here."

Before Jenny could thank her, Mrs Block put a finger to her

lips and cocked her head towards the door. Mr Block and Aunt Clara were coming back, the latter with the navy guernsey draped over her arm.

"Clara say she can mend that, Liza," Mr Block announced, looking like a handsome pirate as he stood grinning in the doorway.

"I reckoned she might do," said Mrs Block. "I ain't seen the hole yet could beat Clara Lovett. Best darner in Newbrigg! Allus was and allus will be, I reckon. We ought to send you round to her for lessons, Leila."

"I'd have to be some clever to darn like Miss Lovett," Leila murmured, raising her head to smile fleetingly.

Suddenly Jenny had the feeling that this scene, or one like it, had been acted many times before, with the Blocks making flattering remarks and Aunt Clara standing, with a smug little smile on her face, having her ruffled feelings smoothed. It was almost as though . . . But that was absurd, she told herself. Why would people like the Blocks be afraid of a harmless little old maid like Aunt Clara?

Yet an hour later she was to wonder if she had been all that wide of the mark. Aunt Clara, in high good humour, had made their supper of toast and cocoa as soon as they returned from the Blocks, then had lit Jenny's candle for her, given her a dry peck on the cheek and sent her upstairs to bed. But Jenny was not in the least sleepy. She lay for a while counting her blessings – Mrs Harris's prescription for a good night's sleep – and thinking how well the day had ended after such a miserable start. Then, feeling as wide awake as ever, she slipped out of bed and tiptoed across the bare floorboards to the window. Pulling the curtains back she saw a sky stippled with stars, and suddenly remembered Josh telling her that at this time of the year flocks of birds were passing overhead all night making for their winter homes, and that their calls could often be heard though they were miles above the ground. She gently raised the sash-window a few inches. Immediately the tangy, sweet smell of the salt-marsh filled her nostrils. Sad, lonely sounds came out of the night. Funereal croaks. A plaintive cheeping.

Distant wails. Whistling sighs. Then, down below in the garden next door, a cheerful, reassuring human noise – Mr Block whistling as he moved about outside his scullery door.

"Liza! Give us out them empty baskets, my darlin'," he called softly to his wife.

Mrs Block must have come out into the yard, too. For, a minute later, Jenny heard her say distinctly, "I don't fare to be able to settle, Bulldog, worritin' about that child nex' door. She's the very spittin' image of her mother. That's bound to upset Clara."

Bulldog stopped whatever he was doing. "If there'd bin any danger of that, Ted would never have left the gel there," he declared.

Mrs Block sniffed. "Ted's like all you men," she said. "Can't see his nose in front of his face. An', besides, he's bin away fourteen year. Reckon he's forgot how odd Clara is."

"Oh, she's not so bad," Mr Block said tolerantly, working at his stacking again.

"There's another thing, too," his wife went on. "That jest come to me five minutes ago. Do you know that's exactly twenty-five year ago this month since it happened, Bulldog."

There was a silence. Then Mr Block said slowly, "Corblast! Is it really? Twenty-five year! That don't seem hardly possible."

"There's more than me will remember," said Mrs Block. "I bet Ted does. And Clara. She's bound to. I hope that don't upset her too much, that's all." Her voice faded as she went back indoors. Then a door slammed.

Jenny pushed the window down and closed the curtains. She climbed back into bed and lay on her side, pulling her knees up and crossing her arms because she was shivering. She did feel tired now, but she could not fall asleep. Figures kept dancing through her brain. Twenty-five years. 1880. Dad would have been fourteen. Aunt Clara must have been ten. Twenty-five years. What did it mean? Was Aunt Clara really odd? Mrs Block had said she was. But then Mr Block had said Aunt Clara wasn't so bad. What a muddle!

When she did finally fall asleep, Jenny had a dream where her father was laughing and saying, "Such a fuss about nothing, Jenny! Such a silly fuss!" The dream was still vivid in her mind when she woke the next morning, and the conversation she had overheard between the Blocks seemed to become part of it. She still felt curious about what Mrs Block had said. She was still determined to ask her father what it meant when he came home. But she was no longer worried by it. Indeed, by the time she was ready to go up to Galaxy House, so excited was she by the thought of her first lesson with Mr Hanley that she had almost forgotten it.

Chapter 7

The rain was falling in slanting strokes against the window and Mr Hanley was sulking because he thought that teaching the cook's niece was beneath his dignity. That was what Jenny felt as she sat at the end of his desk working furiously through the test he had set her. There were five sheets of questions – on English grammar, arithmetic, history, geography and French – and, from the instructions at the top of them, she guessed they were part of a school's entry examination.

"See what you can make of these," he had ordered her forty-five minutes before, dropping the papers before her with an exasperated sigh. It was only too apparent that he did not expect her to make much of them and Jenny, encouraged by Josh's surreptitious winks and grimaces, was immediately on her mettle.

"I'll show him!" she told herself, though she could not help but feel some trepidation as she picked up the papers. As soon as she looked at them, however, she was reassured. She had covered all this ground with Miss Grant early last term. Now, as she reached the mid-point on the final paper (the French one), Mr Hanley left Josh and came over to scrutinize Jenny's finished sheets.

"Well, well!" he exclaimed after a moment. Jenny looked up to find that he was smiling down at her. "So Mrs Gale was right. You *are* a bright young lady. Josh!" he called over his shoulder. "You'll have to give yourself a shake, old man. You can't have a girl making you look a fool!"

Josh smiled amiably enough. But Jenny felt worried. She needed Josh's friendship. She hoped Mr Hanley would not antagonize him by always holding her up as a shining example. Then, at five minutes to ten, Mr and Mrs Gale appeared unexpectedly in the schoolroom. Jenny suspected that they had been arguing, for Mrs Gale's mouth was buttoned-up and her face was rather pink, while Mr Gale had a hard, bright expression in his eyes, the blue of which was accentuated by his bronzed skin and white hair and moustache.

"I've just heard that you have acquired another pupil, Mr Hanley," Mr Gale said. He crossed the room in a few rapid strides and stood, hands clasped behind his back, looking from Josh to Jenny. He was half a head shorter than the curate and only a couple of inches taller than Mrs Gale, but he seemed to be looming over everyone in the room.

Mr Hanley's creamy face went red. "Yes, indeed, Mr Gale," he said with an uneasy laugh. "It was Mrs Gale's idea. I think it might work out rather well."

"I see. You don't think it might look strange, a boy of his age having a little girl for his companion, when he ought to be roughing it at school with other chaps?"

"Jenny Lovett is not a little girl, Wilfred. She is twelve years old," Mrs Gale pointed out testily. She was standing staring out at the rain-blurred·chestnut tree and did not turn her head as she spoke.

"And she is much further on than Josh in her studies," Mr Hanley said.

"Who isn't?" Mr Gale gave a bitter laugh. "You'd never believe I'd spent a fortune on the boy's education. I don't know where he could have been standing when brains were being handed out." He stared gloomily at Josh who, red to the tips of his ears, was gazing fixedly at a page in his arithmetic book.

Jenny's heart went out to the little boy. Although Mr Gale made her feel painfully nervous just by standing there, she decided she must speak up for Josh.

"Excuse me, Mr Gale," she said in a breathless voice, her heart pounding as though she had been running a race, "but Josh learned his French verbs very quickly when I listened to him yesterday."

Mrs Gale swung round and beamed at Jenny. "There, Wilfred!" she said triumphantly. "If Josh must be educated at home in the meanwhile – and Dr Buchan said he must be – he needs the stimulation of a bright, sensible companion. Think how dull our tutors and governesses would have found us had we had no brothers and sisters to share our lessons."

Mr Gale shrugged his shoulders, then checked his pocket-watch against the clock on the mantelshelf.

"Very well, my dear," he said crisply. "Just so long as the boy doesn't turn out a complete muff! And now, if you will excuse me, I have a brewery to run."

Josh leaped up and scurried across the room to open the door for his father, who thrust past him without a word.

Beastly man! Jenny fumed inwardly.

"It's not really me Father dislikes," Josh told Jenny that afternoon, raising the subject of his own accord as they came back into the schoolroom after dinner. "At least I don't think so. I mean if, by some fluke, I sail well, or hit a six in a cricket match, he couldn't be jollier. But he always wants his own way, you see. And he usually gets it, even with Mother – I mean she's wanted a motor-car for simply ages, but he'd rather buy a new boat, so she hasn't a hope. So it's because I'm not doing what he's planned for me that he's furious. Apparently, when I was born he was over the moon, thinking that I'd be the kind of chummy, devoted son to him that he was to his father. I must be a frightful disappointment."

"But not to your mother," Jenny pointed out kindly.

"No. I'm just a nuisance to her. I heard her tell Mrs Buchan one day that no woman of fifty should be burdened with a schoolboy son. She's much more interested in Freda and Margot."

Jenny felt quite shocked. Not so much by Josh's talking about his parents so candidly, but by the resigned way in which he accepted what he thought were their feelings towards him. There had not been a trace of self-pity in his voice. She was still pondering what to say to him, when he said, "I'm afraid I'll have to leave you for a little while, Jenny. I won't be long, though."

A fusillade of rain, driven before a stiff sou'westerly, rattled against the windows as Josh walked across to his bedroom door.

"Another bit of private business?"

"That's right," Josh ignored the mockery in Jenny's tone. "Can you amuse yourself here while I'm gone?"

"Looks as though I'll have to," said Jenny stiffly. "But what do I say if your mother comes up? Or anyone else for that matter? I'm supposed to be keeping you company. That's why I'm here."

"Oh, Mother won't come near," Josh assured her. "She never does. If she's not entertaining in the drawing-room, she'll be paying calls. Your aunt goes home at two o'clock. And Catchpole hardly ever stirs from the kitchen in the afternoon. She eats all the leftovers and ogles the tradesmen that call, in the hope of catching a husband. Anyway, I won't be long. Truly!" he finished placatingly as he disappeared into his room.

He left five minutes later, wearing yellow oilskins and long boots.

Wherever can he be going on a day like this? Jenny wondered. Surely not on the river. She put more coal on the fire and was just debating whether she should light the gas lamp, it was so gloomy, when she heard footsteps on the back stairs.

Her immediate instinct was to hide, and she darted across the room and out into the corridor, closing the door softly behind her.

There was a loud knocking. Then a voice called impatiently, "Master Josh! Are you in there? Your mother want you to come down and meet Mrs Howton."

The door from the back stairs creaked open and Catchpole walked heavily across the room. Jenny did not wait for her to come into the corridor, but ran as noiselessly as she could to the door at the far end and let herself out on to the landing. Her first thought was to hide in the guest room, but she found, to her dismay, that it was locked. Then she remembered Josh's late grandfather's room. That, at any rate, would not be occupied. Its door opened off a little alcove at the head of the staircase, and, when Jenny tried it, it yielded. With a heartfelt sigh of relief she slipped inside.

For a good five minutes Jenny leaned against the door, straining her ears for any sound on the landing. Only when she was certain that Catchpole had not followed her did she begin to breathe freely again and take stock of her surroundings. It was much the grandest bedroom she had ever been in. But then, she reflected, she had never known a family who owned a brewery. The bed was of a type new to her, with a frilled canopy over it, from which chintz curtains hung. The mahogany wash-stand, too, was extremely fine, with four drawers and ruby-coloured tiles along its back.

Jenny recalled Josh's saying that the room had been left just as it was when his grandfather died three years before. But it was certainly not the gloomy mausoleum she had envisaged. On the contrary, everything in it – floorboards, furniture, mirrors – was polished and gleaming. On the blue-and-red patterned wallpaper, photographs and paintings of yachts hung at three different levels. The two largest paintings were above the fireplace. One was labelled "The Schooner, *Starflower*, 1865". The other, "The Cutter, *Moondrop*, Racing off Felixstowe, 1880".

The fireplace faced two tall windows that looked out on to

Wall Road and across the marshes. Through the third window – the largest one – Grandfather Gale must have been able to gaze out to sea as he lay in bed. To the left of the sea-facing window, in the corner, stood a mahogany cabinet of an unusual design. The top part was like a dressing-table with a triple mirror and three narrow drawers. Beneath the drawers was a broad shelf with a rail running round it, probably to protect the three model yachts which stood on it.

On the top of the cabinet, in front of the mirror, stood two framed photographs, each with a black crape rosette attached to the right-hand corner. Jenny, her curiosity aroused, tiptoed across to look at them more closely. The one on the right was of two very pretty girls in old-fashioned dresses, with a slim, curly-haired schoolboy standing between them. The girls' deep-set eyes and the boy's determined chin reminded Jenny straightaway of Josh. Someone had written their names beneath: *Annie, Gerald, Muriel*. And beside them, in a small, neat hand, *They died young*.

The other photograph was of a small, stout woman wearing a dress with a bustle and smiling with stiff self-consciousness. *Dear Sister Dora*, Jenny read. *Faithful to the end*.

She looked at the three bright young faces again. What had happened to them, she wondered. Diptheria? Scarlet fever? Consumption? Mrs Harris had lost three brothers with consumption. How sad life could be. When she wrote to Mary she must tell her about Annie, Gerald and Muriel.

When Jenny returned to the schoolroom ten minutes later she was still wearing the solemn expression she and Mary had always assumed when they walked around the cemetery reading the sad verses on the headstones. But it was not long before she cheered up, for she suddenly spied a Latin grammar book in the bookcase and remembered what Mr Hanley had said that morning: "We'll start you on Latin soon, Jenny, and see if you make a better job of it than Josh has. Perhaps he'll try harder, with you to encourage him." She carried the dog-eared blue book over to the fireside-chair and began to thumb through it.

Josh stared at her in amazement when he came panting in at three o'clock, with the water dripping from his coat and sou'wester. "Lummy!" he exclaimed. "You do have a funny way of amusing yourself."

Jenny ignored this. "Catchpole came up. Your mother had sent her," she informed him. "I had to hide."

"Oh, crikey! Sorry, Jenny!" He hurriedly took off his oilskins and boots and carried them into his bedroom. "Where did you hide?" he asked as he re-emerged, hopping on his left foot as he tied his shoelace.

Jenny was about to tell him, when she checked herself. In retrospect it seemed the most awful cheek to have walked into Grandfather Gale's bedroom without a by your leave.

"I went out into the corridor," she said, carefully avoiding telling a lie.

"Gosh! Good thinking! I don't want Catchpole carrying tales. I don't like her much. Do you?"

"No. I don't!"

"She used to kick our old dog, Captain. And I told Mother in the end. Catchpole's never liked me since."

"She didn't like me from the word go," Jenny told him.

"Well, never mind her. Do you want a tour of the attics? I thought of it on the way home."

"Yes, please."

They spent an enjoyable hour in the big attic nursery which lay above the schoolroom, and which contained the kind of toys at which Jenny had often gazed enviously through the windows of Hamley's and the Doll's Home in Regent Street.

"Lucky you!" said Jenny, taking a last look round before they left this treasure-house.

"Not really," said Josh. "I never had anyone to play with, for a start. Margot and Freda were too old. And this place used to give me the creeps, especially on a windy day." He walked ahead of her, through a long room that was half-filled with trunks and boxes, and out of the door at the far end.

56

"Crikey!" breathed Jenny, staring wide-eyed at the enormous model yacht, on its railed-off platform, which occupied three-quarters of the next room.

"It's a model of the *Windhover*," said Josh. "She was Grandfather's favourite cutter. They built this down in Field's boatyard. But a man came down from London to carve the figures of the crew. Look! There's Lucky Fulcher. He was only twenty-two then." He pointed to the figure standing by the mast, wearing yellowing ducks, and a greyish-white jersey and hat with *Windhover* embroidered on them in red.

"He's looking at me very suspiciously," said Jenny, peering at the wooden face.

"That's because you're a girl," Josh told her with a grin. "I expect he hates it when Catchpole comes bumbling by here with her candle, knocking against the platform." He pointed to a door beyond the yacht's bows. "That's her lair in there. There used to be three other servants, but we got rid of them when Freda and Margot left home, so Catchpole has the servants' room all to herself. Come on," he added, "we'll go back downstairs now and I'll show you Grandfather's room."

Jenny felt very uncomfortable as she ran down the back stairs behind Josh. She hated deceiving him. But she could see no way out of her predicament. She felt it would only make matters worse if she confessed to him now that she had already been in his grandfather's room. Then, as they passed from the schoolroom into the corridor, Josh suddenly broke into a trot.

"I'm just going on ahead to open the curtains," he called over his shoulder. "You don't want to be falling over the furniture."

"But . . ." Jenny checked herself just in time. There! she thought. I almost gave myself away. It's true what Mrs Harris used to say about weaving a tangled web.

Josh was waiting by the open door to usher her into the room.

"Grandfather lay in bed for two years here," he told her, "crippled with rheumatics. I used to have to come up and read

57

to him." He pointed to the hanging bookshelves beside the bed-head. "He kept his favourites in there. They were mainly logs of his cruises when he was a young man and he knew them all by heart. I soon did too. I suppose I was reciting them, not really reading. The best one was the log of the *S S Aurora*, where they went to Russia and saw the Czar. A lot of it was pretty dull stuff, of course. But I didn't mind. I liked Grandfather Gale. He was the last grandparent I had left. Grandmother Gale died when my father was nine. And I never knew my mother's parents . . ."

Josh chattered on, but Jenny was paying him scant attention. She was gazing bemusedly at the top of the cabinet in the corner. The photographs with their crape rosettes were no longer there.

Of course Josh had moved the photographs. That was why he had hurried on ahead on the pretext of opening the curtains. But why? Jenny was still puzzling over this later that evening as she and Aunt Clara set out for one of Mr Waspe's lantern-lectures being held in the chapel.

"Have you ever been in old Mr Gale's room, Aunt Clara?" she asked suddenly.

Her aunt gave her a mistrustful look.

"No, I have not," she said. "I'm the cook, gel. Not the housemaid. Catchpole grumble about it some, though," she added. "She have to clean it thoroughly every Friday mornin'. Then Mr Gale (Mr Wilfred Gale, I mean), he inspect it afterward. Devoted to his father, he were."

"Did he have any brothers and sisters? Mr Gale, I mean – Josh's father."

Jenny could almost feel Aunt Clara stiffen, as she said primly, "Now, look here, gel. The Gales is my employers. An' it's allus bin my rule not to discuss them with no one. That include my own niece. A gossipin' tongue can lose the best servant her job."

"Yes, Aunt Clara," Jenny sighed.

The chimes of the town-hall clock came floating over the glistening roof-tops into lamp-lit Chapel Street. It had not rained for two hours, but the air still smelled damp.

"Eight o'clock!" Aunt Clara quickened her already brisk pace. "Let's hope Amos don't start on time."

As they passed the end of Gun Row, a cold gust of salty wind slapped their faces and Jenny had a glimpse of a rectangle of dark ocean, speckled with the lights of passing ships. She thought of her father, out somewhere on that same black sea, and immediately longed to see him. But before she could become really miserable they arrived at the chapel and she was hustled upstairs to the gallery by Aunt Clara, where they found two seats on the bench behind the Blocks.

The lecture was on the Brightway Scheme for Child Emigration. To begin with, Mr Waspe showed slides of different scenes in the Brightway Home for Orphans and Widows' Children, which brought approving murmurs from the audience. Then he went on to tell the story, illustrated by slides, of a brother and sister, called Dicky and Lavinia.

Dicky and Lavinia had come to the Brightway Home when they were eight and eleven. There were several photographs of them, just after they had been admitted, looking ragged, dirty and very glum. Pictured a few weeks later, however, they were clean and neat and looked almost happy. Perhaps this was because they were going to be sent off to Canada. (Or perhaps it was before they knew, Jenny thought cynically.) But whatever Dicky and Lavinia had felt about it, every stage of their journey – with Dicky in his sailor-suit and Lavinia in her cape and tam-o'-shanter – had been recorded for posterity. There were slides of them waving good-bye to the Home; waiting for the Liverpool train; boarding their ship, the *Maria Merry*; arriving at the Reception Home near Toronto; playing beside a lake with pine-clad mountains in the background.

"And that, my friends, all happened four years ago," Mr Waspe wound up in the deep, resonant voice that made him such a popular preacher. "Here is Lavinia today. A bonny young woman of fifteen who works in a Christian household in Montreal looking after three dear little boys. And here is Dicky, a healthy young lad of twelve, picking apples on the fruit-farm where he lives in British Columbia."

Through the applause that followed, Jenny heard Charlie Block say indignantly to Robert, "That were wholly mean, sendin' them to different families!"

But no one else seemed to think so. Mr Waspe looked over his spectacles at the sympathetic audience and smiled benignly.

"It so happens," he said, "that Mr William Brightway is an acquaintance of mine. So, my friends, if you should feel moved to contribute a trifle to help his valuable work, I shall see that he receives it within the next few weeks. There is a collecting-box on the table in the entrance-hall."

Aunt Clara was dropping sixpence into the box five minutes later, when Mrs Waspe suddenly emerged from the kitchen at the rear of the hall and came hurrying forward.

"So this is your niece, Clara," she said. "We thought so. We noticed her in the High Street. We weren't sure, though." Her reedy voice matched her colourless appearance. Jenny thought. She was a grey person. Grey hair. Grey eyes. Grey dress.

"Yes, Harriet," said Aunt Clara. "This is Jenny. My brother's gel. She don't look much like him, though."

Mrs Waspe put her hands on Jenny's shoulders and peered into her face. "I hope you appreciate what Clara is doing for you and your father," she said. "Your aunt is one of the most self-sacrificing people Amos and I have ever met. But we do feel she is taken advantage of sometimes. Try not to be too much of a burden to her."

"She won't be no burden, Harriet. She's a good, clever gel," said Aunt Clara, pink and simpering.

"I hope so," said Mrs Waspe with a deep sigh.

The nosy, interfering old cat! thought Jenny furiously as she set off for home with Aunt Clara and the Blocks. What right has she to call me a 'burden'? And Aunt Clara playing up to her, too!

Her temper was not improved by the fact that Charlie, Robert and Lizbeth Block (Leila was at home looking after Samuel and the baby) were deliberately keeping their distance from her.

The smell of frying fish wafted out of the dark alleys. High above, an invisible flock of birds passed overhead, calling a plaintive "wee-ooo, wee-ooo". A stranger in a strange land, that's what I am, thought Jenny. And a great surge of loneliness almost took her breath away. Then she felt someone grip her arm, and, looking up, she saw that Mrs Block had fallen behind the others to walk with her.

"I expec' yer dad's missin' you some, Jenny," she said kindly, then added quickly, "but that won't be long till he's back home with you for another little while. Jest about two an' a half weeks that mus' be now till he come home."

Immediately Jenny felt immensely cheered up. She even managed to smile at Mrs Block.

"You haven't forgot what I said, 'bout you comin' round to see me," Mrs Block went on in a low voice. "You're welcome, my dear. Any time."

"Thank you. I'd like to," said Jenny. She meant it. Mrs Block was obviously putting herself out to be friendly. And Jenny felt that she badly needed some new friends. To fill up all the gaps, she thought wryly.

Chapter 8

Perhaps it was her Lovett blood asserting itself, but it was as though, every day, the memories Jenny had of London – of Latimer Gardens, of Laurel Park School, of Mary and her other friends – became more indistinct and fragmented, like the cattle on the marshes when the evening mists came down and their bodies gradually disappeared until they finally shrank into invisibility. She wrote one letter to Mary and

Mary wrote one to her, and though their letters were chatty in a funny way they only seemed to emphasize the distance that had already grown between them.

The mists persisted all through September, woolly-white in the morning, in the evening irradiated golden by the dying sun. Jenny, wakened by the starting-bell from Field's boatyard, or sometimes even earlier by the guns of the wild-fowlers, would stand at her window and watch Lizbeth and Samuel Block running along the marsh track with their mushroom-baskets until they vanished into the white air. Mists meant fine days.

"And there won't be many of those left," wheezed Mr Ball, the baker, who had a barrel chest which made noises like a harmonica. "Clara's usual, is it?" And Leila Block would fetch one of the penny, day-old loaves from the board in the corner and hand it to Jenny with a flickering smile.

Jenny, who started her lessons with Josh at nine o'clock, ran down to the shops every morning at eight to buy what Aunt Clara needed. Normally she went only to the baker's, to Denny's the grocer's, and to the dairy on the corner of Vine Alley on the other side of the High Street. The butcher she never visited, since all the meat they ate came from Galaxy House. But if, for any reason, she had to go further along the High Street – to Abbott's, the draper's, perhaps, or to the cobbler's – she always crossed over before she came to the chemist's so that Mrs Waspe would not waylay her. She had done so once before and, by harping on Jenny's good fortune and Aunt Clara's selfless kindness, had left Jenny depressed for the rest of the morning. It was not very pleasant to be made to feel like a charity case, Jenny thought sourly.

Her chats with Mrs Block, on the other hand, usually cheered her up. She had been returning from the shops one morning just as Mrs Block came running out into the road to shout after Robert who had forgotten his dinner-bag. As Mrs Block turned to go back indoors she noticed Jenny.

"Fancy a cuppa?" she asked pleasantly. "I jest brewed some fresh."

After that, Mrs Block poured out a cup of tea for Jenny at half-past eight every morning and came to hunt her out if she failed to turn up. Jenny learned a lot during these twenty-minute conversations in the Blocks' kitchen, while baby Lucy sat on the floor, happily shaking an old tobacco-tin with a pebble inside. Mr Block, she discovered, was what was called a longshore fisherman.

"That mean he fish along the shore – well, a few mile out, to be exact. He's got his own boats – small ones. At the moment he trawl for sole, but come October he'll be herrenin'. Then sprattin' after that. Of course when the weather's too rough he have to look elsewhere for a livin'. He go eel-pritchin' along the dykes. Or wild-fowlin'. That ain't an easy life. But I'd rather have him doin' that than bein' on a drifter."

"Why?" asked Jenny, stiffening. "Is drifting very dangerous?"

"Oh, no! Bless you, no, my darlin'. I didn't mean that. I were thinkin' of the money. Las' time Bulldog went on a drifter – that were six year ago on the *Snowgoose* – he come home after an eight-week trip without hardly a penny. They'd had such poor fishin' the crew had barely earned their keep, so the owner couldn't pay them nuthin'. That left us in some fix, I can tell you!"

Mrs Block also filled Jenny in on the background of their neighbours in Mariners Terrace, since Aunt Clara, who regarded gossip as one of the deadly sins, had hardly told her more than their names.

Lotty McQueen, who lived at Number One with her old father, Fred Wilson, and her three-year-old daughter, Meg, had been deserted by her soldier husband, and had to work in the net-factory while old Fred minded her child.

The Gochers at Number Nine had come down in the world. They had once owned a boatyard, but Mr Gocher drank 'suffin' chronic' and sometimes burst out into the road, cursing and hollering, while his poor old wife wept and pulled at his coat-tails.

Granny Fulcher had been such an old tyrant that not a girl in

Newbrigg had wanted her for a mother-in-law, so Lucky, her only child, had remained a bachelor. Old age had mellowed her, however. "She read tea-cups an' tell fortunes," Mrs Block told Jenny confidentially. "The young gels swear by her. But don't never mention that. She could get took up afore the magistrates if the wrong folks heard of it."

"Take care, or you'll turn out like my mother and her friends," Josh warned Jenny, when he heard about her morning tea with Mrs Block. "The Newbrigg gossip-shop, that's our drawing-room on a Wednesday afternoon. You can hear them from halfway down the drive. Like a flock of roosting starlings."

"I'm only acquiring local knowledge," said Jenny, affronted.

Josh groaned. "You never stop acquiring knowledge. Who's Mr Hanley's golden girl, then? Who never lifts her nose from her desk all morning? Who's a disgusting bluestocking?"

"I enjoy lessons," Jenny told him. "Just the way you enjoy birds."

"But you enjoy birds, too, now. I've taught you that. I bet you'll be grateful to me one day."

It was true. By now she could recognize many birds she had never known existed before she met Josh. She could distinguish a yellow-crowned widgeon drake from his dull brown mate and the noisy, long-legged redshanks from the similar-looking, but much quieter, knots. But she knew she would never have the patience to lie stock-still for an hour, as Josh did, on some old sacking at the edge of the North Marsh waiting for a reed-warbler to emerge.

The first time Josh took her to the North Marsh she saw immediately that he was happier there than on the river. The expression in his eyes as he looked around him was one of total content. She soon discovered why.

"Do you see what's so marvellous about this place, Jenny?" he said. "There's no real cover. So they don't shoot here. The birds are left in perfect peace."

One day they walked along Wall Road, past the station, to

the golf course, at the edge of which was a belt of fir trees. There Jenny found herself looking through Josh's binoculars at dozens of birds, some rose-red, others greyish-green, swinging upside-down on the high branches and tearing at the pine cones.

"Crossbills," Josh told her, grinning at her amazement.

On another sunny afternoon he left her to practise her rowing by the old jetty, while he went off in the punt on one of his mercy missions. When he returned he looked so sick and white that Jenny insisted they go straight home, where, ignoring Catchpole's surly glances at having her privacy invaded, she made him a cup of tea and added half a teaspoonful of brandy to it.

But, although they had so quickly become good friends, Josh still regularly slipped away on his own to attend to his private business. This began to irk Jenny. "Friends don't have secrets from one another," she told him once, tight-lipped. But he became conveniently deaf. She understood how Mr Gale felt when confronted by Josh's silent stubbornness. She told herself angrily that she was going to follow him when he went off on his next excursion. But she never did.

Sometimes, during morning lessons, while Mr Hanley was correcting her exercises, she would study Josh as he wrote his answers, cheek almost touching the paper, tongue sticking out of the corner of his mouth, and would suddenly feel afraid for him. What if this private business of his were more than just a boy's game? What if it were dangerous? He could be quite a foolhardy little boy. Look how he had lain out on the roof of his school. He might have died from that. And his parents knew nothing about it.

Jenny had been shocked when she had learned how little Josh's parents actually saw of him, and that the only time he ate with them was when he joined them for dessert in the evenings.

"Rich folks' ways," Aunt Clara had said. "They don't want young 'uns around when they're entertainin' guests. That's the long an' the short of it."

"Then I'm certainly glad I wasn't born rich," Jenny declared, thinking nostalgically of the companionable meals she, her father and Mrs Harris had enjoyed together.

Aunt Clara was proving less difficult to live with than Jenny had feared. True, she was strict about Jenny doing her chores – half an hour's darning or sewing in the evenings and collecting driftwood and sea-coal from the beach on Saturday mornings. And she insisted on three attendances at chapel on Sundays. But there seemed no basis for the fears Jenny had overheard Mrs Block expressing. Indeed, if anything, Aunt Clara had a weakness for showing Jenny off and boasting to neighbours like old Mrs Fulcher about 'Edward's clever gel'.

"I'll ask Dad to tell her she's making me conceited," Jenny decided, after one particularly embarrassing encounter. "That should stop her."

Mr Lovett was due home on 8 October and Jenny was eagerly ticking off the days in her almanac till his return. Then, on the morning of 3 October, a Monday, the postman leaned down from his cart with a letter for her, just as she was leaving to go along to Galaxy House. Recognizing her father's handwriting, she ran back indoors and tore the envelope open.

He was not coming home! That was the news that hit her between the eyes, two-thirds of the way down the page, after she had read about his seasickness, how his wrists had been badly chafed with hauling and how dogfish had been biting great lumps out of the nets and the herring. 'Bob Blowers wants me to stay on permanently as mate,' he had written. 'Great news, really, poppet! But we'll be going straight into the Home Fishing when we get back to Lowestoft. So I won't be able to come down to Newbrigg until the end of November. Don't be too downhearted, though. We'll be in Lowestoft harbour every Sunday until late afternoon. So if Aunt Clara brings you up on an early train, we can have most of the day together. Tell her I'll be sending some money soon, and give her my love . . .'

Jenny ran round next door to quickly tell Mrs Block the news. She gamely tried to hide her bitter disappointment and put on a cheerful face because her father had found a permanent berth. "And at least I'll see him once a week, on Sundays," she finished brightly.

At the time she could not understand why the smile vanished from Mrs Block's face to be replaced by a look of apprehension. She was to find out at five o'clock that afternoon.

"Journeyin' on a Sunday!" said Aunt Clara, staring at Jenny as though she had suggested robbing a bank. "Never!"

"But I must!" cried Jenny. She could feel her eyes starting out of her head and the skin tighten on her temples. "You can't keep me away from my father. You don't know how I was looking forward to seeing him again. You don't know how I've been missing him!"

Aunt Clara did not open her mouth. Her expression was wooden, as she turned away to fill the kettle.

"What's wrong with travelling on Sunday?" Jenny demanded, following her aunt to the sink. "We wouldn't be working."

"We'd be making other folks work, which is jest as bad."

"Then I'll go there on my own!"

"That you won't! A young gel like you! You're in my charge for the time bein'. An' you'll do what I say."

"Oh, please, please, Aunt Clara! Don't make me wait till the end of November to see Dad!"

"No journeyin' on a Sunday! An' that's final!"

"Then I won't come to the rotten old chapel with you on Sundays. And you needn't try to make me!" cried Jenny, distraught, as she rushed out of the kitchen and upstairs to her room. "Wild horses wouldn't drag me!"

"An' we know who that is talkin'," Aunt Clara called after her in a tremulous, high-pitched voice. "That heathen that took yer father away from us all. Blood will out, they say."

Of course, as Jenny realized later, the Blocks must have heard the commotion, just as she and Aunt Clara heard the

67

Blocks' noisy squabbles or hilarity. So it was no coincidence that Mrs Block arrived at the door at seven o'clock, ostensibly to return a cup of sugar she had borrowed.

"All right are you, my mawther?" she enquired so solicitously as she came into the kitchen that Jenny, who had been fighting back her tears for two hours, immediately broke into noisy weeping.

"I jest knowed this would happen! Jest knowed it!" Mrs Block cried, putting motherly arms around Jenny, when she had heard her sorry tale. "You'd never git Clara Lovett to move anywheres on a Sunday. Not if her life depended on it. You'll jest have to resign yersel', my poor little owd darlin'. Yer dad's surely forgot what Clara's like . . . But you can write to him now, at least, him bein' in Lowestoft," she finished consolingly. "He'll be some pleased to hear about yer lessons with Mr Hanley."

"Mrs Block," said Jenny, as soon as she was in control of her voice, "why did Aunt Clara speak about my mother like that?"

Mrs Block held Jenny at arm's length and shook her head. "Her spittin' image, you are, Jen," she sighed. "That's half the trouble, I should think." She looked thoughtful for a minute, then took a deep breath as though she had come to a decision. "Well, I can't see that'll do any harm to tell you," she went on, "but make us a good strong cup of tea first, my love. Nuthin' like tea to lubricate the old tonsils, as my mother used to say."

While Jenny was infusing the tea, Mrs Block lit the lamp and set it down in the centre of the table. Then, cradling her cup in her hands, she looked straight at Jenny. "Truth of the matter is, yer Aunt Clara thought yer dad was goin' to marry her," she stated abruptly.

"My father! Marry Aunt Clara!" Jenny exclaimed, disbelievingly.

"Well, he weren't yer father then, love," Mrs Block pointed out with a faint smile. "He were jest a good-lookin', kindhearted young man, who had bin Clara's champion from the time she came to live with the Lovetts at eleven. Ted would

never let any harm come to Clara. An' she whoolly worshipped the ground he walked on. Trouble was, he never guessed
how her feelin's were takin' a romantic turn. Yer grandmother
did, though. An' she encouraged it. She'd have bin only too
pleased to hev had Clara fer a daughter-in-law.''

"But she's so plain and dowdy!" Jenny burst out.

"That didn't trouble yer grandmother," said Mrs Block.
"She were lookin' fer a good wife fer her son – one that could
cook an' mend an' manage money. Clara could do all that.
They said Alfred would hev had her willingly. But it was yer
father her heart were set on. Trouble was, he were so bloomin'
kind to her she thought he felt the same way she did. She were
jest waitin' fer him to name the weddin'-day when yer mother
come on the scene.''

"Did you know my mother?"

"Not to speak to, my darlin'. I seen her about, of course,
when she were nursemaid to them toffs at the hotel. An' once
when yer father brought her here after they was married. Very
pleasant-lookin' young woman, I thought. But I reckon the
Lovetts never gave her a chance to be pleasant to them. They
jest didn't want to know her. So she never came again.''

Mrs Block drank another half-cup of tea, then stood up.
"Well, I'd best be gittin' back," she said, "otherwise that
bunch of mine'll be drivin' poor Leila up the wall." She paused
in the kitchen-doorway and turned to look earnestly at Jenny.
"Take a bit of advice from me, love," she said. "Try not to rile
yer Aunt Clara. She's had a lot of trouble in her life, an' she can
act some funny at times. You don't want to be a-stirrin' up
trouble – for yer dad's sake as well as yer own.''

Jenny lifted the lamp from the table to light Mrs Block along
the passage. As they reached the front door, she said suddenly,
"Where did Aunt Clara come from? I mean, if she was eleven
years old when Dad's family took her in . . ." She looked at
Mrs Block enquiringly.

But for once Mrs Block was unwilling to talk. "I'm sure I
don't know anythin' about that," she said hastily, pulling the
door open. "I were only a young 'un then myself." With a

brief, "'Night, Jen," she had hurried away down the path, banging the gate shut behind her.

But she does know, thought Jenny shrewdly as she walked slowly back to the kitchen. She just doesn't want to tell me. She would ask her father, she decided, when he came home at the end of November. The end of November! Almost two months away. An eternity, she thought drearily.

Perhaps Aunt Clara had had time to reflect on how unhappy Jenny must be feeling, for when she came in at eight o'clock she was obviously making an effort to be amiable. Jenny, remembering Mrs Block's advice, decided to cooperate.

"Shall I fetch the work-basket?" she asked politely.

"Yes. Do! There's a sheet needs patchin'," Aunt Clara said. "I'll show you how to do it. We'll make a needlewoman of you yet, gel."

"Yes," murmured Jenny and forced herself to smile for her father's sake.

Chapter 9

Jenny, standing heavy-hearted at her bedroom window on the morning her father had originally planned to come home, watched Mr Block walk down his back path, then, somewhat to her surprise, disappear into the lavatory which stood beside the shed at the foot of his garden. Up until that moment she had assumed the lavatory was an old one, and not in working order, because the family only seemed to use the other one which stood back-to-back with Aunt Clara's.

She was about to take her winter coat from the wardrobe before going to gather Aunt Clara's fuel from the beach, when she gave a gasp and leaned forward. Yes! Her eyes had not deceived her. There were thin threads of smoke wisping up from the tiled roof of the old lavatory! As she watched, the threads thickened and became columns.

She pulled up the window. "Mrs Block! Mrs Block!" she shouted excitedly.

But the Blocks' scullery-door remained closed. Then Jenny remembered that, since it was Saturday, all the children would be at home and there was probably such a hubbub in the kitchen no one would hear her.

"Mr Block! Mr Block!" she called as loudly as she could, for by now the smoke was coming out in wicked little puffs from several different parts of the roof. But there was as little response from Mr Block as there had been from his family.

The door must have jammed, she thought in a panic. He has somehow set himself on fire and now the door has jammed and he can't get out!

Jenny had never moved so quickly in her life. She was out of the room and down the stairs in six great leaps, almost twisting her ankle as her boot slipped off the bottom step. Within seconds she was hammering on the Blocks' front door and pushing it open before Charlie – who had come running along the passage – could open it.

"Quick! Quick! Your lavatory's on fire and your father's inside!" she shouted.

Charlie gulped. "Mam! Mam!" he yelled, diving back along the passage to the kitchen. "She says the lavvy's on fire! An' Dad's in there."

"Who says?" Mrs Block swung round in alarm, clutching the baby to her chest.

"Her from nex' door."

As Jenny pushed past Charlie, who had frozen in the doorway, Lizbeth began to scream. Mrs Block shook her impatiently as she bawled, "Whatever is it, Jenny? What's wrong?"

"Your lavatory's on fire! And Mr Block's inside."

"Oh, Dad! Dad! My Daddy!" Little Samuel, sobbing, flung himself against his mother.

"Save him! We must save him!" Robert almost pushed Samuel and Lizbeth over in his desperation to reach the back door.

The others, with Jenny following, tumbled out into the backyard after him.

"Where's the fire then?" Mrs Block gasped, staring in bewilderment at the lavatory that backed on to the Lovett's.

"There, Mrs Block! There!" Jenny's shaking hand pointed towards the garden's end. "Oh, look! The smoke's getting thicker. He'll be suffocating! Do something. Quickly!"

"Oh, my godfather! Jenny!"

Jenny stared at Mrs Block in horror, thinking the shock had unhinged her, for, with the baby perched precariously on her right arm, she was supporting herself against the scullery wall with her left hand and tears were rolling down her cheeks.

But then Charlie suddenly flung himself on the ground, braying like a donkey and thumping the earth with his clenched fist, and Robert began to stagger round with his arm across his forehead, hooting like an owl.

Samuel, swinging on his mother's skirt, looked up at the sky and tried to bray like Charlie.

Only Lizbeth stood stock-still, making no sound. Then, all at once, she came marching up to Jenny, her small, tear-stained face pink with temper, and said furiously, "You great owd stoopid dicky, you! That's not a lavvy! That's the fish-house where Dad smoke his herrin'!"

"I could have sunk into the ground!" Jenny told Josh on Monday, as they stood in the yard after their lessons, watching Jeremiah Double lead Bess the pony out to the trap which was to take Mrs Gale along to the Rectory for lunch. "Especially when Mr Block came out to see what the noise was, and nearly choked to death laughing when they told him. Still," she added, "there's one good thing. The young Blocks have all become quite friendly now."

"Good," grinned Josh. "And now wait till you hear my news! Mr Hanley told Father on Friday evening that my work's improved no end. So the old Pater's given me back all my bird books. And not only that! He says if I go on improving, I'm to have a very special Christmas present this year. And I just bet it will be a camera. Because he knows I want a camera more than anything in the world."

What Jenny wanted more than anything was to have her father home again. But she had to be content with writing him two long letters a week, using the pages of an old exercise-book that Josh gave her. Mr Lovett wrote his letters on Sundays, one to Jenny and one to Aunt Clara. Aunt Clara's, Jenny was happy to see, were always much shorter than hers. Indeed she was tempted to ask her aunt whether she felt it right to read letters that had been written on the Sabbath. But, remembering Mrs Block's advice, she held her tongue.

Mr Lovett's letters to Jenny were full of humorous stories about what had happened on the drifter the previous week. How, for example, George (the workhouse lad that Bob Blowers had taken on as apprentice) had made a gallon jug of tea, forgetting to put the half pound of tea in with the water, milk and sugar; how the cook's Norfolk dumplings had exploded all over the galley, and how, on George's first night on board, Sidney Hunt, the third hand, had been down in the rope-room, coiling the rope as the nets were hauled in, and had finished the job with his face as black as his oilskins from the soot of the lamp. "Please, sir. What's the Indian gentleman called?" George had whispered to Mr Lovett as Hunt came up on deck.

What Jenny's father did not tell her about were the rough seas, the autumn gales and the many occasions when the drifter was within a hair's-breadth of disaster. But, living with Aunt Clara, Jenny could not for long remain ignorant of the hazards he must be facing on every trip. For her aunt would often sit during their evening mending sessions lugubriously recounting the tragic ends of local boats and local fishermen, including those of Grandfather Lovett and Alfred. Then she would progress to more macabre stories, such as the one about the ship that was found, one wintry morning, in the breakers off Newbrigg beach, with the bodies of her crew lashed to the mast, each one encased in a block of ice.

Sometimes, as she listened to Aunt Clara, fleeting recollections of Latimer Gardens, the shop, Mrs Harris and Laurel Park School would pass through Jenny's mind. More and more these were like blurred images from some dimly remembered dream. Even Mrs Harris (from whom Jenny had not yet received a letter – not knowing where her permanent home in Glasgow would be, she had left no address with the Lovetts) was becoming a remote figure. It was as though Jenny had lived in Newbrigg for years, battling along to the shops in the morning in the teeth of the screaming east winds, and waking to the deadly boom of a punt-gun from the marshes, or the crack of a rifle from the shore. She felt as if she had never been taught anywhere else but in the Galaxy House schoolroom, with the windows rattling in the gale, the logs crackling on the fire and Mr Hanley's sing-song voice explaining Pythagoras's theorem, or the river system of East Anglia.

Jenny stood once in Neptune Row with Josh watching the waves leaping and snarling on to the promenade, while the spindrift rolled about at their feet like great yellow cauliflower-heads. For some reason she suddenly remembered a gigantic traffic-jam she and Mrs Harris had encountered in the Strand, and about which people had talked for days. She could not now imagine why they had thought it so important.

One Wednesday morning, around the middle of October, the lifeboat gun went off while Mr Hanley was giving them a lesson on Mary Tudor. He ran down with them to the beach and they arived as the crew, some still being helped into their oilskins by their wives, were clambering into the *Laura Smythe*. Jenny soon found that there was no point in trying to talk, for the noise was tremendous. The wind howled and thundered across the shingle while, at the bottom of the beach, huge waves exploded like cannon. Through the clouds of spray she had occasional brief glimpses of the distressed ship (a German barge, they learnt later) lying at an angle on the sandbank where it had struck. Then a part of the large crowd that had gathered helped shove the lifeboat into deeper water with the thirty-five-foot-long launching pole that normally hung on the side of the shed. Jenny closed her eyes as she saw the bows of the boat submerged by a steep wave and the yellow sou'westers vanish. But when she opened them again the *Laura Smythe* was a hundred yards out and her sail was up. Half an hour later she beached safely with the rescued men and Jenny, Josh and Mr Hanley returned to Mary Tudor. It was not until that evening that Jenny discovered Bulldog Block had been one of the crew.

"Aren't you afraid when your father goes out in the life-boat?" Jenny asked Leila one evening as they walked along the beach.

"Oh, yes," said Leila in her small half-whisper, "but he got to do it. That's his duty."

Since the day of the 'fire', Leila had taken to calling round for Jenny after tea. If the evening were fine they would go down to the beach and watch Mr Block's boat go out, with Charlie or Robert sitting forward of the pile of brown herring-nets and Mr Block and his brother rowing furiously. A little way offshore the sail would go up. Then, in the gathering dusk, they would see the lights springing up all over the purply-black sea, where the longshoremen were fishing.

Leila was an amiable enough companion, but so shy and diffident that Jenny was often irritated by her. Even when they went to see the Trafalgar Centenary procession on 21 October, with its decorated floats and marching bands, Leila hardly opened her mouth. Jenny could not help comparing her unfavourably with Mary Moore, or even with Josh. Both Mrs Block and Aunt Clara, however, were delighted with what they saw as a budding friendship.

"You won't go wrong, do you stick with Leila Block," Aunt Clara said firmly. "She's a good, quiet, hard-workin' gel with no funny ideas in her head."

"Yes, Aunt Clara," sighed Jenny resignedly.

She would not have risked upsetting her aunt by telling her that Leila Block bored her. Since their quarrel about visiting Mr Lovett, they had both been taking pains to avoid any unpleasantness. Despite what she had said, Jenny had gone to chapel as usual on Sundays and Aunt Clara had shown no surprise at this. Every day was bringing Mr Lovett's home-coming a little nearer and life was gliding along fairly smooth-ly – until Aunt Clara had her nightmare.

Monday, 24 October, had been a raw day with an easterly wind and occasional bursts of icy rain. Jenny's room was as cold as a morgue and full of draughts, so that by the time she had said her prayers, kneeling by the side of her bed in her nightgown, she was shivering so violently her teeth rattled. She dived into bed, blew out her candle and hugged the flannel-wrapped hot brick which Aunt Clara placed in her bed every night. Then, winding the heavy quilt round her body, she was soon warm and comfortable enough to drift into a dreamless sleep.

When she awoke, the blackness seemed to press down on her. There was not a glimmer of light, not even through the crack where the curtains did not meet, so she knew it was nowhere near dawn. Then, as she rolled over on her side, wondering what had disturbed her, she heard the scream. It catapulted her out of bed and had her standing, shivering, on the bare floorboards, almost before she realized what she was doing.

Any sudden, severe fright had always caused Jenny to turn sick and faint. Now, true to form, she broke out in a cold, prickly sweat, and her ears began ringing. "I won't faint! I won't!" she told herself furiously and sat down heavily on the bed, leaning forward so that her head was between her knees. After a minute the nausea and giddiness passed, and she sat up and fumblingly lit the candle that stood on her bedside-table.

As she walked across to open the door her shadow jumped in the draught, as though in fright at a long-drawn-out wail, which was, if anything, more bloodcurdling than the scream-ing. Jenny took a deep, quivering breath, strode across the landing and walked resolutely into her aunt's bedroom.

The candle-flame leaped this way and that, so it was a

moment or two before Jenny made out the figure kneeling on the bed, hands covering her ears, her face turned up towards the ceiling. Well, at least she's not being murdered, Jenny thought, relief making her legs quite wiry for a moment. She had been imagining drunken old Mr Gocher gone berserk and clambering in windows to attack his neighbours. Even so, her heart lurched unpleasantly as Aunt Clara wailed unnervingly again. Her eyes were wide open, but it was obvious that she was still asleep. Jenny knew from Mrs Harris that a sleep-walker could die of a heart-attack if woken suddenly. And, although Aunt Clara was still in bed, the same might apply to her.

She leaned over the bed and put a hand gently on her aunt's bony shoulder.

"Aunt Clara! Aunt Clara!" she whispered. "It's Jenny. Wake up, Aunt Clara!"

Aunt Clara turned her head, blinked, then, seeing Jenny, whimpered and shrank away.

"Aunt Clara! It's me!" Jenny said, a little more loudly.

"Jenny? Jenny Lovett?"

"Yes. It's me. You've been having a nightmare."

Her aunt gave a groan, then sank back against her pillow, her arms crossed over her flat chest. Jenny could see that she was trembling violently.

"You *are* in a state!" said Jenny in concern. "I'd better make you some hot milk."

She quickly lit the candle on her aunt's bedside-table, ran to her own room to pull on her coat, then hurried downstairs into the cold kitchen. She poked the glowing embers of the range into a blaze and put a pan of milk on to heat. The clock on the mantelshelf stood at five minutes to two. By quarter-past two, Aunt Clara had drunk the milk and seemed quite calm.

"You're a good gel, Jenny Lovett," she said in an exhausted voice, as Jenny prepared to go back to her own room. "You're kind-hearted, like yer father."

Having left her aunt on such terms, Jenny was totally

unprepared for the reception she met with at seven o'clock the following morning, when she came sleepily into the kitchen to ask Aunt Clara how she was feeling.

"Fine," said Aunt Clara, turning from the range to stare at Jenny. "How should I be feelin'?"

"I thought you might be tired . . . after your nightmare," Jenny said awkwardly.

"Nightmare!" Aunt Clara glared at her. "What you talkin' about? I never had no nightmare!"

"Yes, you did! You were screaming. Don't you remember? I made you hot milk."

"You did nuthin' of the sort," said her aunt with a contemptuous laugh. "It's you that's bin dreamin'!"

"I wasn't," cried Jenny indignantly. "You were screaming and wailing. And when you woke up you were shaking like a leaf. You *must* remember!"

"Don't you tell me what I mus' do!" Aunt Clara advanced a few steps, brandishing the poker. For a moment Jenny really believed she was going to strike her, for she looked quite mad. "You've got some nerve, I mus' say! Tellin' lies about me to my face. An' don't let me hear that you've bin tellin' other folk this fairy story neither! For if I do, I shall punish you!" She turned away and attacked the smouldering fire fiercely, rattling the poker against the iron bars.

Jenny looked at the dresser. The cup with the yellow roses on it – the one she had used for Aunt Clara's hot milk last night and had left in her room – was back on its hook. Aunt Clara had brought it down and washed it. She must know that Jenny had been telling the truth. For the first time Jenny felt real scalp-prickling fear as she looked across at the bowed, black figure in front of the range. But the real danger, though she did not know it, lay in her not having read correctly the expression on her aunt's face. For that had been one of fear, too.

78

Chapter 10

On 27 October, a letter arrived for Jenny from Mrs Harris, enclosing a card to be forwarded to Mr Lovett, whose birthday was on the twenty-eighth of the month. Jenny felt immensely cheered at hearing from their old friend, even though her news was not entirely happy. She had arrived in Glasgow to find her brother suffering badly from asthma and living in a damp, unhealthy flat. Consequently she had had to start house-hunting straightaway and had only recently found a suitable two-room and kitchen on the south side of the city looking out on to a park. As soon as they were settled in, she would send Mr Lovett and Jenny her address, she promised, so that they could write and tell her their news.

That evening, with Aunt Clara's permission, Jenny untied her father's birthday parcel (which contained another guernsey from Aunt Clara and an embroidered bookmark from Jenny) and slipped Mrs Harris's card inside. Then she tied it up again so that it could be posted next day. She had been afraid that Aunt Clara might be jealous of Mrs Harris's having remembered Dad's birthday, but was surprised to find the reverse was true.

"She sound whoolly good-hearted!" Aunt Clara exclaimed, when Jenny had read out the old housekeeper's letter. "Takin' time to think of Edward, with all them troubles of her own! But I allus did like the Scots. Of all them hundreds of Scotch boats that come down to Lowestoft for the Home Fishin', there's not one ever sail out on the Sabbath."

It was Aunt Clara's unpredictability that Jenny found most unsettling, for there seemed no rhyme or reason to the woman's moods, particularly since the episode of the nightmare. Quite often Jenny would look up and find her aunt's prominent brown eyes fixed on her – almost fearfully, she thought.

"But I'm sure she wouldn't harm me," she told herself firmly. "She wouldn't hurt a fly. She's a good, God-fearing woman. It's true she's peculiar. But so are lots of people. There were children at Laurel Park School who had drunken mothers or fathers. And they had to live with them always. I only have to put up with Aunt Clara for another nine months at most. So I expect I'll survive."

Still, she had to admit that she would be glad when her father came home, so that she could find out exactly what lay behind Aunt Clara's strangeness.

The Waspes certainly did not appear to like Aunt Clara any the less for her being a little odd. Indeed, it seemed they could not have enough of her company. Jenny found this out the following Sunday evening, when Aunt Clara called her into the parlour. Jenny always sat in the kitchen when the Waspes came round, reading the only books Aunt Clara allowed her – the 1888 and 1889 volumes of *Sunday Reading for the Young* – so she had never had the pleasure of seeing Amos and Harriet Waspe sitting stiffly side by side on the horsehair sofa, drinking tea from Grandmother Lovett's wedding-china cups and staring thoughtfully at the leaping, blue-green flames of the driftwood fire.

Mrs Waspe waited until Aunt Clara had left the room and closed the door behind her, before she spoke.

"Well, Jenny," she began in her flat voice, "you have been here almost two months now . . ."

"Six and a half weeks," Jenny corrected her.

". . . almost two months," Mrs Waspe repeated, as though Jenny had not spoken. "You must feel perfectly at home now in Newbrigg." Her pale eyes widened interrogatively.

"She must do. Quite at home. Quite secure. With Mr and Mrs Block close at hand too. Salt of the earth," Mr Waspe muttered, looking over the rim of his teacup at the shining toes of his black boots.

Jenny could not think where this conversation was leading.

80

"Yes," she agreed warily. "I'm quite used to it now, thank you."

Mrs Waspe sighed contentedly, as though Jenny's admission had been a point won.

"Well, in that case," she said, leaning forward a little and looking up earnestly into Jenny's face, "you would not mind being left here on your own for a weekend?"

"On my own?"

"Your Aunt Clara has never had a holiday," Mr Waspe said reprovingly, as though this were somehow Jenny's fault. "My wife and I are going to the Brightway Home in Surrey on 11 November and we have been invited by William Brightway to bring a guest. We thought immediately of poor, dear Clara."

"She has permission from Mrs Gale for a weekend away, but she is worried about leaving you here on your own," Mrs Waspe added in a whisper, as though she suspected Aunt Clara might be listening at the keyhole. "She did not want to broach the subject with you herself, in case you became worked up about it. Poor Clara cannot stand unpleasant scenes. You do realize that?"

There was an insinuating note in her voice that made Jenny flush. "Well, I'm sure I don't want to stand in Aunt Clara's way," she said shortly. "I'll manage quite well on my own. I'm not a baby."

She did not miss the quick exchange of glances which she knew was a silent comment on her rudeness. But she was unrepentant. It was infuriating to learn that Aunt Clara was giving people the impression that it was Jenny who had temper-tantrums.

After that evening, however, there was a decided improvement in the atmosphere in the house. Aunt Clara's forthcoming holiday occupied her thoughts to the exclusion of all else and Jenny was no longer subjected to her brooding stares. She bought a smart black dress from Madame Edie's at the select end of the High Street, and she sat, every evening, close to the lamp, sewing frills of broderie anglaise on to a set of new, snowy-white undergarments, meanwhile telling Jenny, again and again, every detail of the train journeys that Mr Waspe had planned for them.

"An' I hope there won't be no trees blow down across them railway-lines!" she would invariably finish, looking up anxiously from her needlework as the wind, raging in the blackness outside, gripped the kitchen window and tried to rattle it to pieces.

There were continuous high winds. Indeed, Jenny almost forgot what it was like to be able to walk along a road without either bending double, head into the wind, or leaning backwards against its insistent shoving. Mrs Block said that there had never been such a bad start to the spratting season for years. The sea was so rough that it was impossible for the men to go out, and some of them were in the Beach Company shed every day, gambling away the money they had made at the 'herrenin''. Not so Mr Block. He was out eel-pritching along the ditches most afternoons, or doing odd jobs for the owners of the large villas along Wall Road.

Jenny dared not think how her father was faring.

"Put dark thoughts out of yer head, my mawther," Mrs Block advised her. "Fishermen's families have to. Otherwise we'd all be stark starin' mad."

On 5 November, for one whole day, the gales miraculously abated. It was the Tercentenary of the Gunpowder Plot, so a more elaborate celebration than usual had been organized. Round the corner, on the drying-green, was a huge bonfire, whose girth had been increased daily by pieces of driftwood cast up by the rough seas. The fireworks, though, were set off from barges in the middle of the river. Despite the wind having fallen it was a bitterly cold evening and Aunt Clara hustled Jenny off home at nine o'clock. Josh, however, was allowed to wait on the quay until the finish of the display at ten and he consequently caught a cold. He ought to have stayed indoors the following week, but the rough weather was driving ducks of all kinds to the shelter of the river and the wild-fowlers were out daily in full strength. This meant that Josh's mercy missions had to become daily events too.

Then on Friday, 11 November (the day Aunt Clara, in a state of tremulous excitement, set off by train with the Waspes for Surrey) the gales which had been coming from the north-west for five days suddenly changed direction and began to blow in from the sea. When Jenny looked out of her bedroom window at half-past eight, she thought it had snowed. Then she saw that thousands of seagulls had gathered on the mar-shes. That afternoon she and Josh stood by the Beach Com-pany shed watching great clouds of lapwings coming in over the sea and dropping down to settle beside the gulls. The wind was shrieking in their ears and the spray from the huge, exploding breakers peppered their cheeks like pellets. Jenny, noticing a line of figures along the river-wall, silhouetted against the grey sky, shook Josh's arm and pointed to them.

"They're looking for any weak points in the wall," he yelled in her ear. "If this wind keeps up there will be flooding tonight at high tide. The water will surge up the river and try to break through the wall. When that happens it flows right across here and meets the sea coming over the shingle bank." His face was pinched-looking and anxious as he gazed over the marshes.

Jenny felt a stab of fear. It would be ironic if there were flooding on the very weekend she had been left on her own! But then, as they turned and headed back towards the town, she remembered that she was to eat her tea at the Blocks and could stay there until bedtime if she wanted. So she would be less on her own this evening than she normally was.

Along the promenade men were battling to fix up window-shutters and stout, protective doors on the vulnerable sea-facing buildings. The fishing-boats had been pulled right up on to the footpath. And when Jenny and Josh turned up Vine Row they were swept along before the wind like balls of spindrift.

Josh had a bad coughing fit as they came out on to the High Street.

"Look here," he said when he could talk, "I feel a bit groggy. I think I'll go home, Jen."

"Ask your mother to give you some medicine," Jenny told him. "I think your cold's worse today."

"I shan't see Mother until tomorrow," he said disconsolately. "She's playing bridge with the bank manager's wife and her cronies. And Father's going there straight from the station to join them for dinner. There's just crabby old Catchpole at home. And I certainly won't ask *her* for medicine. She'd give me arsenic for spite."

Jenny thought of Josh that evening as she sat in the noise and warmth of the Blocks' crowded kitchen. As usual the Blocks were eating red herrings and swedes for tea. All the children were wearing hand-me-down clothes. They probably did not have a dozen toys among them. Yet they were far better off in many ways than poor little Josh. They always had their mother with them for a start – and they had one another, too. Jenny had noticed at tea-time how Charlie helped little Samuel with the bony parts of his fish; how Robert kept a piece of cake on his plate for Lizbeth, who was a slow eater and might otherwise have missed out, and how Leila, in her quiet way, helped look after them all, untying stubborn pinafore-strings, fastening awkward buttons and wiping sticky fingers.

By seven o'clock the gale seemed intent on blowing the house down. Mr Block, his wind-flayed face like a red sun beneath his black sou'wester, looked in to warn them to be ready to go up to the church with their blankets and their food in about an hour's time.

"River-wall's been breached already," he shouted over his shoulder as he hurried out again.

Jenny was beginning to feel sick with nerves. Every few minutes she yawned, which was a sign of nerves, too. Mrs Block must have noticed. For she suddenly called from her fireside-chair, "Don't you be a-worritin' now, Jenny. The lads'll shift yer aunt's stuff upstairs. They allus do. An' you'll be perfectly safe here with us."

At quarter-to eight she told Jenny and Leila to go next door and fetch Jenny's quilt to take up to the church. Leila carried the storm-lantern, and, as Jenny held the gate open for her, the older girl pointed meaningfully towards the High Street. There was no talking above the screaming wind, but Jenny understood and nodded. They linked arms and, with heads lowered, fought their way down to the end of Wall Road. For once, the Jolly Mariners was empty and silent. As the girls reached its corner they were almost blown off their feet. When they turned into the High Street, however, they found the going easier. They came to a halt on the corner of Vine Alley. Across the road was Vine Row, and, at its further end, in the fitful glimpses of moonlight, Jenny could see an ominous white band flowing towards them, then drawing back. Forward. Back. Forward. Back. But each time it advanced it was a little closer. Fear hugged her until she could hardly breathe. She was looking at the enemy creeping remorselessly nearer and nearer. Without a word she and Leila linked arms again and turned to run back the way they had come.

When they reached Aunt Clara's, Leila stood halfway up the staircase, holding the lantern high, while Jenny fetched her quilt. Then they hurried to the safety of the Blocks' kitchen.

At five-past eight Mr Block strode in, grinning.

"As you were!" he called. "Tide's on the ebb. Water's goin' down."

The boys, who had been waiting excitedly for the word to leave, wailed in disappointment. For a minute Jenny could almost have joined them, the sense of anti-climax was so great. But she was glad enough to creep into her bed at half-past nine, knowing that the kitchen beneath her was still dry and warm.

Other parts of the town had not been so lucky, as Jenny discovered when she ran down to the shops for her bread and milk the next morning. Down Vine Row, Neptune Row and Gun Row, teams of labourers were shovelling shingle into carts and house doors stood wide open as their occupants swept out the noxious-smelling mud.

After she had had her breakfast, Jenny set off with her basket to gather fuel and found that both River Walk and the drying-green were covered with a layer of shingle and mud. There was still a stiffish breeze blowing, but the sun was breaking through and she decided to walk as far as the look-out tower. She had reached the corner of the net factory when her eye was suddenly caught by a bright splash of colour in the shingle piled up against the wall. She walked across to investigate and, a moment later, stood looking sadly down at the lifeless bundle of blue and chestnut feathers which she gently placed in her basket. She was pretty certain that she had found Josh's roller. The only consolation was that it appeared to have died naturally, for there was no sign of any wound.

Jenny had no intention of risking an encounter with Mr Gale when she was carrying a dead bird in her basket (particularly when it was the bird that had lost Josh his race in the regatta!), so, even though it was Saturday and she was not expected at Galaxy House, she ran round to the back door and quietly let herself in, praying that Catchpole would be busy in the dining-room. Her luck was in. The kitchen was empty. She tiptoed quickly across to the back stairs and hurried into the schoolroom, where she expected to find Josh. But, though it was half-past nine, there was no sign of him. Then Jenny remembered his cold and wondered whether he had been confined to bed. She went over to his bedroom door and knocked. There was no answer, but she thought she could hear people murmuring. She knocked again, then cautiously pushed the door open.

What she saw made her eyes shoot wide open: Josh was asleep – sprawled, fully clothed, boots and all, across his bed – and, every time he breathed, his chest made muttering, whistling noises. Jenny turned cold with foreboding when she realized the state he was in. The legs of his trousers and the sleeves of his jacket were caked thickly with mud; his oilskins and sou'wester lay in a pool of water beneath the window where he must have dropped them, and there were two more little puddles beneath the toes of his boots, which were dangling over the edge of the bed. Lying on the floor, just inside the door, was his untouched breakfast tray, left there by Catchpole.

She hasn't even tried to wake him! thought Jenny angrily. And I know why! She thinks that if he doesn't appear downstairs, his father or mother will come up to look for him. And if they find him like this there will be ructions!

She leaned over the bed and shook the boy roughly. "Wake up!" she whispered urgently. "Wake up, Josh!"

He rolled over on his back and stared up at her vacantly. His face was flushed and his hair damp with perspiration.

"Josh! What have you been doing?" Jenny wailed. "If your parents find you in this state, they'll hit the roof!"

He struggled to sit up, his eyes glittering feverishly. But the effort was too much. He flopped back again with a groan and rolled over on his side.

"You are a little fool!" Jenny raged. "Going out when you had a bad cold already, in that terrible storm . . ." Then she stopped in dismay.

Josh had caught sight of the dead bird in her basket and had started to cry. The tears were rolling down his flushed cheeks and he was shaking with great shivering sobs. She knew then how weak and ill he must be feeling. For Josh never cried – not even after the most harrowing of his mercy missions, no matter how fiercely his father shouted at him.

"I'm sorry," she said tremulously. "But I thought you would want to see it. It is the roller, isn't it?"

He nodded, taking a grip on himself and dashing his tears away with his muddy cuff. "Will you throw it in the sea for me?" he asked in a painfully hoarse voice. "When the tide's going out? I couldn't bear to think of it buried."

"Of course I will," said Jenny calmly. She was trying to imagine how Mrs Harris, who was the most sensible person she knew, would have behaved in this situation. "Now, listen, Josh," she went on cheerfully, "we must get you out of those dirty, damp clothes straightaway. Sit up and lean against me . . . That's right . . . Your chest sounds almost as musical as the baker's today. Come on! No need to be silly and shy. I'll turn my head away. Where's your nightshirt? Under your pillow? There you are, then. Don't take all day about it!"

Once Josh was in bed, she quickly mopped up the pools of water with the towel from his wash-stand, then shoved it into her basket along with all his damp, dirty clothes.

"I'll ask Mrs Block if she can clean these for you," she told him. "We can trust her not to ask questions."

Josh gave the ghost of a smile. But when Jenny leaned over and put her hand on his forehead, she found it was burning. She suffered a brief spasm of panic at the thought that he might be seriously ill, but managed to say, calmly enough, "I'm going down to ask your mother to come and have a look at you now. But don't worry. No one will know you brought this on yourself. Catchpole knows, of course, but she can't very well tell tales now."

She was turning away when Josh gripped her wrist with fingers that felt like hot wires against her skin.

"Listen, Jenny," he croaked, his chest whistling alarmingly, "I need your help. I can't ask anyone else. And it's urgent. But you mustn't tell anyone about the matter I want you to take care of for me. It's a deadly secret. So you mustn't tell anyone at all. Will you promise?"

Jenny looked at him doubtfully. She did not believe in giving blind promises.

"Please, Jenny!"

She could not refuse, when he was so ill. "All right," she said. "I promise."

"Good." Josh's breathing was becoming noisier by the minute. "Now, listen carefully. I have a friend that I help. He lives down on the marshes in the old Shepherd's House. To get there you go through the white gate opposite the look-out tower and along the path that leads to the river-wall. Just before you reach the wall, you'll see a track going off to your left across the marsh. There's a ditch on either side of it. It runs dead straight, so even if it's covered with a few inches of water (and it might be today) you won't lose it. Just keep going straight. The house is at the end of it on a piece of rising ground. Tell him I sent you. His name's Godwit. Say that you've come to help instead of me. Go this afternoon around two. The water should be down by then."

"But what do I have to do?" Jenny began to ask. Josh had fallen back on his pillow. His eyes were closed, and he was making a snoring noise.

Jenny ran across the schoolroom, along the passage and down the front stairs, her basket swinging wildly. Then, dumping it in the porch, she raced over to the dining-room to alert Mrs Gale. As she left, both Mr and Mrs Gale were running up the stairs.

So that's Josh taken care of, she thought. And now I'm left with Godwit. Who can he be? A cripple? A blind boy? An invalid? What an odd name to have given anyone! She knew what godwits were. Josh had pointed out plenty of them. Seagull-sized birds with long legs and pink-and-brown bills. Was Godwit the boy's Christian name, or his surname? And why was Josh so determined to keep him a secret? Would Mr and Mrs Gale disapprove of him?

But I will know this afternoon, she reflected, as she hurried down to the beach to dispose of the poor roller and quickly collect Aunt Clara's firewood.

He was a little old man with grey bushy eyebrows and side-whiskers and he wore a torn jacket and old, patched, moleskin trousers. As soon as he spoke, Jenny knew that she liked him, because his voice was soft and warm and full of concern for Josh. He had been brushing out the last of a stinking, puddingy mixture of mud and shingle from the downstairs room when she squelched up the path, calling (so as not to startle him) that she was Jenny Lovett come from Josh Gale to visit Godwit.

"I'm Godwit, my mawther," he told her with a faint smile. Then, suddenly realizing the significance of what she had said, he added sharply, "Suffin' wrong, is there? Is young Josh poorly?"

89

When Jenny nodded, the old man's eyes clouded. "Oh dear!" he sighed. "I was afraid this would happen. He got wet through las' night when he were helpin' me. An' the water were still knee-deep along the track when he went off home. Do he fare to seem bad?"

Noting the tremor of anxiety in the old man's voice, Jenny tried not to sound too pessimistic. "I think his cold's just gone to his chest," she said. "But I shouldn't think they'll allow him out for a while. So he asked me to come and give you a hand in the meantime. If you don't mind, that is," she finished politely.

"That's kind of you," Godwit said gently as he propped the mud-caked brush against the wall, "but I couldn't think of askin' a young gel to help lift them heavy owd cages. That's what Josh were comin' for. I reckon they'll have to stay where they are for the time bein', though."

He turned away and made to step inside. But Jenny (thinking of Josh's dismay if she had to report that her mission had failed) cried, "Oh, please! Mr Godwit. I'm very strong. Just as strong as Josh. And I did promise him that I would help you."

Godwit paused in the doorway and seemed to consider for a moment. Then he half-turned his head.

"All right, my dear," he said good-humouredly. "Seein' as yer so determined, come along inside. Watch yer step, though. The floors is still some slippy."

The Shepherd's House had been built fifty years before and designed to withstand the winter floods. A passage ran through it from back to front with the back door facing the sea and the front door opening on to the river. Last night, as always during a tidal surge, the two doors had stood wide open to allow the sea to rush through in a torrent – doing the minimum of damage to the rest of the house. Jenny could see the water-mark on the passage walls, level with her shoulders. But it was the smell that would not let you forget that the sea had been there. A smell of rotting seaweed and of old, unwashed seashells that had been forgotten and shut away for ages in a closed drawer.

"Phew!" she said, holding her nose.

"I know," said Godwit sympathetically. "That make yer stomach turn. An' that'll linger for days. Still, it could hev bin worse." He shuffled rheumatically ahead of her along the passage and turned into a doorway on the left.

"I brought the little 'uns down, soon as I got this room cleared an' the fire lit," he remarked, as Jenny followed him in. He nodded towards a row of cages, made out of fish-baskets and wire-mesh, that stood before the range. Each held one or two small birds. "Most of those young Josh brought in," he told her, stooping, with a grunt and a sharp intake of breath, to peer into the cages. "We got all sorts. A pretty little shore lark here. A couple of redwings. A snow bunting come down early an' got shot for his pains. Some dunlins. And a dear little goldcrest. They're lookin' a bit droopy cos that were cold upstairs. They like the heat when they're injured, poor little owd things."

He straightened and walked over to give the fire a poke. The room, Jenny saw, was completely bare apart from the cages. And the small window at the back, which faced the sea, had been roughly boarded up.

"All right? Shall we go up now an' fetch down the big 'uns?" Godwit looked at Jenny uncertainly as though he thought she might have changed her mind. When she nodded, he added, "They'll take a bit of manoeuvrin'. That owd staircase is some narrow."

He opened a door to the left of the range and Jenny saw that the stair was indeed narrow – and twisting as well. She followed Godwit as he climbed slowly up with grunts of pain, and went through a doorway at the top into what was obviously his living-room. Bleak enough quarters they were, too, she thought, feeling quite shocked as she saw the table made out of an old door, balanced on bricks, the straw paliasse, with its thin grey blankets, lying on the floor, and the two fish-boxes, covered with sacks, that served for a chair. There was the meagrest of fires in the open grate, while buckets and tins, placed at intervals round

91

the room, showed where the ceiling leaked.

Most of the remaining floor space was taken up by the three big packing-cases which Godwit had converted into cages to accommodate larger birds like the guillemot, the owl and the bittern, which now occupied them. The guillemot was huddled in a corner. It had a broken wing, Godwit told Jenny, but it was mending. The owl (which Jenny could not see, since its cage was covered by a blanket so it would sleep) was a young one which had been shot in the foot. The bittern was wide awake and regarding Jenny with none too friendly an eye. Indeed, as she approached its cage, it began to croak threateningly and suddenly spread out its long breast-feathers into a protective fan.

"Shot in the leg old Bottlebump were," said Godwit, looking down on the bird like a doting father. "An' that were some job puttin' the splints on him, I can tell you! Tryin' to git my eyes an' my face all the time he were, with that owd long, sharp beak of his! Had to put a bag over his head in the end, an' git young Josh to hold him . . . But yer larnin' to trust me, ain't you, owd feller?" he crooned. "You know who bring you yer fish an' yer fieldmice. An' it's for yer own good, so's you can soon be back out in them reeds boomin' to yer lady-love."

Jenny could have sworn the bird understood him. Its eyes brightened, it cocked its head and the angry fan of feathers subsided.

"We'll carry him down first," said the old man. He shuffled over to fetch a blanket from his bed and draped it over the cage. "There! That'll keep the owd boy calm. Now you lift your end, my mawther," he told Jenny, "an' you go down first. Backwards. All right? Take it easy now. That's a good gel. You are some strong! Good as young Josh any day."

He had limitless patience, never scolding when Jenny was clumsy or when she moved the wrong way at the sharpest angle of the stairs, and trapped them there for five full minutes before Godwit managed to work the cage free. She could see him wince with pain as his rheumaticky old joints protested at the manoeuvres he was having to make. But he never complained or raised his voice. And, whenever she looked at him, his gentle brown eyes shone approvingly.

Half an hour later the three big cages sat with the others in front of the range. By this time the small birds had perked up quite noticeably with the heat. And, within minutes of joining them, the guillemot, too, began to look livelier.

"I'll have to go soon," Jenny said apologetically. "Mrs Block might wonder where I am. I told her I was going beachcombing, so I don't want to worry her. Is there anything else I can do for you?"

"No, no, my dear. You run off home. And thank you kindly for yer help. Tell young Josh to look after himself. And say Godwit's thinkin' of him. He were a good friend to me when I were laid up with the fever las' month."

"Shall I come again and tell you how he is?" asked Jenny.

"I'd certainly appreciate it, if that ain't too much trouble," the old man told her.

"Can I bring you anything when I come? Is there anything you need?"

"No, my dear. Thank you fer askin', though."

When she looked back from the end of the track, she saw him out in his front garden digging for the worms that had been washed out of their holes by the flood.

"Of course there are things he needs," wheezed Josh crossly. "He just didn't like to ask."

Although he was still quite ill, he had insisted on seeing Jenny on Sunday evening and Catchpole (to her mortification) had been sent down to the Blocks to fetch her. Jenny found Josh lying propped up with pillows and smelling strongly of camphorated oil in a room made unusually cheerful by a blazing fire, with the gas-lamp above the mantelshelf turned up full. On a small table was a dish containing the ozone paper which was burned twice a day to help his breathing.

"Well, you can tell me what Mr Godwit needs, and I'll take it to him," said Jenny.

"It's not *Mr* Godwit. It's just Godwit," Josh said petulantly. "And he needs food for the birds, of course. I take him a bag of grass-seed twice a week from Jeremiah Double's stock (you'll have to sneak into the shed while he's having his dinner), scraps of meat from the kitchen, and fish-guts from the top of the beach . . . You'll just have to use your commonsense."

"Yes. All right. I will," said Jenny soothingly. "When will he need it?"

"Go on Tuesday," Josh began, then was overcome by a fit of coughing that brought Mrs Gale in from the schoolroom to cut short Jenny's visit.

"But what I would like to know," she said to herself as she ran down Wall Road with her bobbing lantern (for Mr and Mrs Block, Leila and Robert, were waiting for her to go to the evening service with them) "is why Josh helping old Godwit has to be kept such a deadly secret. I mean what harm is the old man doing? With his little bird-hospital?"

Then her mouth tightened. That was probably it! People in Newbrigg shot birds. They did not mend them. Only yesterday she had heard the fishermen on the beach complaining loudly about the gulls tearing the fish out of their nets. And Lucky Fulcher had been ranting to Aunt Clara not so long ago about the terns that nested along the shingle, stealing the fishermen's livelihood. Look at Aunt Clara herself: she stated quite openly that she hated birds, and did not even give a reason. What a bloodthirsty lot they were, with their ten-bores and punt-guns and rifles! Kill, kill, kill! That was all they seemed to want to do. She was glad she did not belong to Newbrigg. The sooner she was back in London among civilized people, the better. Then she thought of the Blocks and her face softened. They were all right. They were good friends to her. Mrs Block had cleaned all Josh's dirty clothes without asking a single question, so that they could be smuggled back into his room as soon as Jenny had an opportunity. And Mr Block was one of the best-natured men she had ever known.

But, at chapel that evening, Jenny received the shock of her life. After the third hymn, several of the congregation stood up to tell how they had been converted. Among them was Mr Block.

"It happened twelve year ago," he began in his strong, cheerful voice. "I were on a drifter going round to the Westward. We struck on a shoal one night and I saw every one of my mates swept away. I were the sole survivor. I swore then I would mend my ways. For afore that, brothers an' sisters, I had bin a great sinner. The demon drink. That's who I worshipped. On his altar I sacrificed my poor dear wife an' my innocent child. They starved because of my drinkin'. An' many a time in my drunken madness, I beat them. But the good Lord reached down his hand that night and saved not just my body, but my soul."

Jenny shrank away from Leila who was sitting next to her. Mr Block's terrible confession had made her feel like sinking through the floor. So how must poor Leila and Robert and Mrs Block be feeling? She glanced fearfully along the row and saw to her astonishment that they were all beaming proudly. Later she discovered that Mr Block regularly gave testimony of his conversion. But Jenny felt that evening as though a prop had been knocked away from under her. She had grown very fond of good-natured Mr Block in the short time that she had known him. Now, in her mind's eye, she kept seeing him as a drunkard and a wife-beater. Even when she sat in his kitchen, later, listening to him play hymns on his melodeon, the darker image of him would not be banished. More and more she was learning that nothing (and no one) in Newbrigg was really what it seemed.

Aunt Clara arrived home at eleven o'clock on Monday morning, shiny-eyed and full of praise for William Brightway, his Home and his Emigration Scheme.

"He's a saint, that man! A real saint!" she kept declaring.

Her weekend away had done her good, Jenny decided. The

furrows had disappeared from between her brows and the sharp edge had gone from her voice. She seemed genuinely concerned that Jenny might have been afraid during Friday night's storm and she was obviously upset when she heard that Josh was so ill.

"I'll git up there straightaway an' make him a jelly to tempt his appetite," she said, hastily pulling on her apron. "You won't be havin' no lessons for a while, I reckon, so I'll have to think of suffin' for you to do in here. We can't have the Devil findin' mischief for idle hands, Jenny!"

Jenny was not too unhappy at the prospect of spending her mornings cleaning or mending for Aunt Clara – anything, so long as she did not have to work again in the Galaxy House kitchen! But, in the event, she was spared even this. For, half an hour later, Mr Hanley arrived at the door.

"Mrs Gale is agreeable. And so is your aunt," he announced without any preamble, as he strode past Jenny into the kitchen, where he dumped a pile of papers on the table. "This is a week's programme of work I've set out for you. We should be back in the schoolroom by the end of the month. But I don't want you falling behind, when you're doing so well."

"Thank you very much indeed, Mr Hanley." Jenny flushed with pleasure.

The curate smiled down at her. "Not at all." And, for the first time – perhaps because he had been roughed up by the wind – Jenny noticed how young he looked. More like a big, red-haired boy than a man. "It's I who should be thanking you," he went on. "You have given me an aim. To do the best I can for you, so that you will be quite ready for your examination when you leave here. It's very satisfying, I find, teaching a bright child like you."

"Thank you," murmured Jenny, blushing again, but more because she was flattered by Mr Hanley's confiding in her, than by his compliment.

"Not that I don't like Josh," said Mr Hanley. "I do. And I sympathize with him, too. About his ornithology, I mean. But I can hardly tell him that, in view of Mr Gale's attitude. I had just the same kind of battle with my father, you see," he finished sadly. "I wanted to be an actor, would you believe? But my family had all gone into the Church. Father, Grandfather, Great-grandfather . . ."

"Jolly decent of him to tell you about it. I shall probably work harder for him now," Josh commented the following Friday afternoon.

It was 18 November, exactly a week after the tidal surge, and Mrs Gale had told Jenny she might go up to see Josh at two o'clock and stay with him until he felt tired. Jenny had smuggled his clothes in under her coat and shoved them into his wardrobe. Now, perched on the foot of his bed, she looked at him consideringly. His face was chalk-white and he had dark shadows beneath his eyes, but he was so obviously on the mend that she thought she might safely ask him some questions about Godwit. Not straightaway, of course – after she had talked to him for a bit. So she told him what Mr Hanley had said. And how Robert Block had been playing truant.

Then she said casually, "Your friend, Godwit . . . Doesn't he have any other names?"

"I don't know." Josh scowled and slid down beneath the quilt.

"Is that a nickname – Godwit?"

"Yes."

"Why is he called that?"

Josh looked at her balefully.

"I believe that, when he was a young man, he killed twenty godwits with one shot. That's what I heard. I've never asked him, of course. I'm not so nosy."

"*Killed* them? Godwit did?"

"That's what I said."

Jenny began to feel a little indignant at Josh's manner. After all, she had not exactly enjoyed stealing Mr Double's grass-seed last Wednesday, or picking up fish-bits from the shingle like a scavenger, or scurrying along by the Beach Company's shed, afraid that Mr Block might be in there and spot her. And she would have to do it all again tomorrow. So surely she had a right to know something about the old man she was helping.

"Hasn't he any friends in the town apart from you?" she asked.

"No."

"How does he earn a living?"

"He's a reed-cutter. He catches eels. And he makes baskets. Now go away, Jenny! You've tired me out with all your questions."

Jenny saw the stubborn set of the boy's mouth as he turned his head crossly away, and knew she would learn no more from him. It was Godwit himself who told her the next day how he and Josh had met.

"I were livin' in my owd houseboat then . . . Look, gel! That's it down there by the wall, next to my owd marsh-boat. D'you see it? I only moved into this place las' year, you see. It's bin lyin' empty since 1900. No one seem to mind me bein' here, so I'm stoppin' till I'm moved . . . Anyways, I were livin' in the houseboat, an' one day I see this little owd lad strugglin' along with a poor wounded heron in his punt. He were a-blarin' some too! Breakin' his little owd heart. (He were only a little chap then.) I hollered to him. An' he come over. Well, I managed to fix that owd bird up in a few weeks. An' Josh an' me have bin mates ever since. Don't hardly know what I'd do without him now."

On 23 November, a Wednesday, there was a chilling, misty drizzle. Jenny had purloined some pieces of raw steak from the Gales' pantry before filling the bag Josh had given her with grass-seed from the big sack in Jeremiah Double's potting-shed. Then, with the lot held awkwardly beneath her coat, she raced down Wall Road just after one o'clock, keeping her eyes averted from Mariners Terrace, in case old Mrs Gocher or little Meg McQueen happened to be at their windows and expected her to wave. The track to the Shepherd's House was unpleasantly slippery and twice, because she was running too

98

fast, she almost came to grief and slipped into the brimming ditch.

Then, as she reached the corner of Godwit's front garden, she heard a high wailing that set her heart bumping with fright. She stood stock-still. But after a moment the pitch of the voice changed and Jenny suddenly realized she was listening to singing – the slurred, unlovely singing that often drifted out of the Jolly Mariners on Saturday nights. Taking a deep breath, she walked resolutely up to the window and looked in. Her lips pursed as she saw the old man sitting stupidly on the floor among his cages, beating time to his drunken song with a half-empty bottle. He looked pathetic and ugly, his face blotched, and his eyes wide and glassy. Jenny felt sick. She crossed over to the door, opened it and flung the bag of seed and the meat on the floor. Then she hurried off home.

"Well? What about it? He has a rotten life. He's full of rheumatics. And he doesn't get drunk very often," cried Josh defiantly, when she told him what she had seen.

But Jenny could see that he was upset, for his face had turned crimson and his bottom lip was trembling treacherously as he pretended to be engrossed in the bird book that was propped up on his knee. She decided that, at least while Josh was still convalescent, she had better not mention old Godwit's weakness again.

Chapter 11

They started on a campaign of baiting Catchpole that last week in November, never dreaming, of course, what it would lead to. To some extent they were both taking their revenge on her. But there was more to it than that. Josh was not quite well enough to be up and about, but he was strong enough to be looking for some outlet for his energies, while Jenny was just suffering from a surfeit of high spirits because her father's homecoming was in sight. So they rang the bell for the housemaid continually.

"More coal, Catchpole!"

"Josh needs fresh water in his jug."

"This glass is dirty, Catchpole!"

"This water isn't warm enough for washing in!"

Catchpole did not dare ignore Josh's bell, for Mrs Gale was still in a state of nervous anxiety about him and insisted that his every whim be pandered to. So the young woman's fat legs clambered up and down the back stairs until they must have ached.

"Serves her right," said Josh. "Mean, spiteful pig! I hope she gets veins."

"Aunt Clara was giving her a real dressing-down when I came in just now," Jenny reported gleefully to Josh on Wednesday. "In front of Jeremiah Double, too! The best fish-knives had been put away dirty. You should have seen Catchpole's face! It was like a great red tomato."

"A burst tomato!" said Josh vindictively, as he swallowed his last mouthful of boiled fish.

Mrs Gale had suggested that, until Josh was fully recovered, Jenny should come up and eat her dinner with Aunt Clara every day at half-past twelve. So she normally arrived at noon, in order to sit with Josh for half an hour, while he ate his invalid food, with many grimaces and exclamations of disgust.

But today Josh had more important matters on his mind than either Catchpole or the demerits of boiled fish. He handed his tray to Jenny so that she could lay it on the floor, then picked up a dog-eared green book that had been lying beneath it.

"I say, Jen," he said. "I want you to do me a favour. This chap here says quite positively that there has never been a sighting of an alpine accentor in the east of England."

"An alpine what?"

"Accentor. It looks like a hedge-sparrow and it lives in the Alps and the Apennines," he explained, adding, "Old

100

Saunders will know, though. He's in the middle cupboard in the bottom of Grandfather's cabinet. Do you think you could fetch him for me? *Manual of British Birds*. A red book."

Jenny looked at him doubtfully. "Are you allowed to have it?"

"Of course I am," said Josh impatiently. "They're very indulgent at the moment. That's why I'm making the most of it."

Poor Josh! thought Jenny, as she ran off across the schoolroom and into the corridor. He probably half enjoys being ill, since it's the only time his parents pay attention to him.

Grandfather Gale's room was exactly as she had last seen it, except for the fact that the two photographs with their black rosettes were back in place. Jenny looked at the pretty girls and the bright-eyed boy.

"Now I can find out what happened to you all," she told them, as she knelt down to open the cupboard.

The *Manual of British Birds* was the only book in it, sitting on top of a pile of yellow magazines.

"I've just rung for the polecat again," Josh greeted Jenny with a wicked grin. "I can't bear the sight of that dirty dish sitting there."

As Jenny handed him the book, she said casually, "Who are those people in the photographs on your grandfather's cabinet?"

She knew from the guilty rush of colour to his face that he had forgotten she was bound to have seen them this time.

"They were my father's brother and sisters. Aunt Dora was Grandfather's sister, and she looked after them all when their mother died," he said shortly.

"I see." After a moment Jenny said, "What did they die of?"

"How would I know!" Josh avoided her eyes and hastily thumbed through Saunders. "Lack of breath, I suppose!" he added sarcastically.

"You must know," said Jenny. "They were your aunts and uncle, after all. Your father must have told you about them. Especially when they all died young, like it says on the

101

photograph. It must be a tragic piece of family history."

"Perhaps people in my family don't like talking about morbid things," said Josh, glaring at Jenny.

They were close to a quarrel when Catchpole came in, red in the face and breathing heavily.

"Oh, there you are!" said Josh coolly. "Could you remove the tray, please?"

As Catchpole stooped, her corsets creaked plaintively and Jenny and Josh spluttered behind their hands. By the time the housemaid had slammed the schoolroom door behind her, their quarrel was forgotten. Josh deftly changed the subject.

"I say," he cried, pushing the open *Manual of British Birds* in front of Jenny, "I was jolly well right. Look at that. An accentor's been seen both at Cambridge and Lowestoft."

Jenny decided to forget about the photographs for the moment. If Josh wanted to be secretive about his family, she certainly did not want to pry.

Then, as Jenny ran downstairs to the kitchen for her dinner at half-past twelve, she met Catchpole on her way up to her room – it was her afternoon off. The housemaid simpered and suddenly shoved a folded piece of paper into Jenny's hand.

"Here," she whispered. "This newspaper-cuttin'll tell you about them in the photographs. You can read that while yer waitin' for yer dinner. Whoolly interestin', that is. Show it to yer aunt too. She'll like to read it."

"Thank you very much," muttered Jenny, taken aback and embarrassed by this sudden show of friendliness.

"Don't mention it," called Catchpole gaily as she went on her way.

Jenny sat down at her usual place at the table, with her back to the range, where her aunt was still busy, and spread the cutting out flat. It was from the *Eastern Gazette* and was dated Friday, 24 September, 1880.

'*Terrible Boating Accident At Newbrigg*', the headline said.

Jenny's eyes widened as she began to read.

'*Our Newbrigg correspondent telegraphed on 23 September as follows:*

*A sailing-boat was capsized here today with disastrous
results. The* Shooting Star, *belonging to the well-known
yacht-owner, Mr Joshua Gale, of Gale's Brewery, was
taken out on the river by three of his children and his sister,
Miss Dora Gale. They had arrived at that part of the river
known as Decoy Reach, when the boat was capsized by a
puff of wind and the occupants thrown into the water.
Master Gerald Gale, eighteen years old, was the only
swimmer of the party, and he made heroic efforts to save the
others. He pulled them, one by one, to the side of the boat
and tried to help them cling to it. No help could be given
from the bank as the disaster occurred too far out. Unfortu-
nately, by the time the screams of the poor people were heard
by other craft, they were suffering so from cold and exhaus-
tion that, in full view of their would-be rescuers, they
slipped, one by one, into the water and were swept away.
The victims of the tragedy were Miss Annie Gale (22
years), Miss Muriel Gale (20 years), Master Gerald Gale
(18 years) and Miss Dora Gale (50 years). Mr Joshua
Gale and his only remaining offspring, Mr Wilfred Gale
(26), were being comforted this evening by friends.'*

"But how dreadful!" cried Jenny, remembering the young,
lively faces in the photograph.

"What is it?" asked Aunt Clara curiously. "What you
lookin' at?" She came forward, still stirring the gravy, to peer
over Jenny's shoulder.

Jenny held up the cutting. "It's about Mr Gale's brother and
sisters," she said sorrowfully. "Catchpole gave it to me."

Aunt Clara gave a little moan. Then there was a crash and a
thud. The crash was the gravy-pot falling on to the hearth. The
thud was Aunt Clara's head striking the fender. When Jenny
turned round and saw the thread of crimson on her aunt's
sallow cheek, she screamed.

"Run for Mrs Gale, gel!" rapped Jeremiah Double who had
just walked into the kitchen.

"Lucky for me," Jenny told Josh later, "or I would have

103

fainted! I always do at the sight of blood. Your mother was on the half-landing, on her way upstairs, when I caught her. She can't half run! When she'd had a look at Aunt Clara, she sent me to fetch Doctor Buchan. My ears had begun to ring by then and my legs felt quite hollow, but after I had made them run for a bit, I felt better. Doctor Buchan brought me back in his motor-car and, by that time, Aunt Clara was sitting up and the blood had been wiped away, so it was all right."

"What did your aunt say?" asked Josh quickly.

"Only that she had turned round too suddenly and had taken a giddy turn. She didn't want to go home and rest, but your mother said she must. Doctor Buchan took her in his motor. Actually, I think your mother just wanted Aunt Clara out of the way. She had seen the cutting on the table and put it into her bag. And she sent Jeremiah Double out while she asked me where it had come from. When I said Catchpole had given it to me, her face turned nearly purple."

"It would." Josh looked very grave. "Catchpole stole that cutting from Grandfather's bureau."

"She said I must never mention the incident to Aunt Clara again – or to anyone else, but I shouldn't think that included you . . . What does it all mean, Josh?"

"I can't tell you," he said. "I would if I could. But just do as Mother says, Jen. Forget it. And, whatever you do, never ask your aunt about it."

He looked so serious that Jenny felt a shiver run down her spine. But there was more unpleasantness in store for her that evening. Aunt Clara, apparently quite recovered, had gone to work as normal, and Jenny was catching up on some arithmetic, when there was a sudden loud knocking at the door. When she opened it she found Catchpole standing there, carrying a carpet-bag, her normally pale face pink and puffy from weeping. The young woman's eyes bulged as though the hatred inside of her was trying to push its way out.

"Jest come to tell you I got my notice through you an' that weasel-faced little brat up at the House," she said, her voice shaking with rage. "You drove me to it, an' don't pretend you didn't. An' I wish you bad luck from now on. The worst luck. Both of you. That's all!'' she finished, turning away to tramp off to the station.

"Catchpole's curse!'' exclaimed Josh, when Jenny reported the next day that Grandfather Gale's room was now locked and she could not replace the *Manual of British Birds*.

Catchpole's curse, thought Jenny heavily, when her father announced that he could only stay in Newbrigg for a week.

Chapter 12

When Mr Lovett came striding along the station platform on Saturday afternoon, his face was so weatherbeaten that Jenny did not recognize him. Half an hour later, seeing how his hand shook as he drank his first cup of tea with them, she sprang to her feet in alarm, thinking he was ill.

"It's with hauling in the nets, poppet,'' he told her with a reassuring grin. "You should see me try to shave.''

"Well, never mind!'' she said solicitously. "Now that you're home, you can have a good long rest.''

That was when he broke the news that he was only with them for a week.

"Bob needs help making up –'' he explained, "– getting everything mended and ready for the next trip. The old gel had a rough time last month. There's spars need attention, nets to be mended, ropes to be gone over and all the floats to be freshly painted. It'll take us all our time.''

"Take me all my time, then, to git yer clothes ready!'' Aunt Clara exclaimed, making for Mr Lovett's bulging duffle-bag as though she would start on his washing there and then.

"Hold on, Clara!'' said Mr Lovett quickly. "Wait till you see the fruits of my labour!'' He drew a little suede bag from his inside jacket pocket and emptied twenty-five golden sovereigns out on to the table. He pushed five of these towards his sister. "Those are for Jenny's keep, as we agreed, so I don't want any nonsense about your not taking them."

Aunt Clara had been about to protest, but, thinking better of it, swept the coins into her apron pocket.

Mr Lovett smiled at them both. "The rest can go into the bank," he said. "It's not a fortune – but I'm fairly pleased with it."

"I would say it's a very handsome pay-off, first trip out after fourteen year, Edward Lovett," said Aunt Clara happily, carrying Edward's duffle-bag into the scullery.

Jenny looked after her thoughtfully. Aunt Clara had never once referred to the events of Thursday – not even to Catch-pole's dismissal. But she had been more than usually moody and withdrawn until Dad arrived. It was as though, just by being there, he chased away all her anxieties, so that by now, even the two little worry-lines between her brows had disappeared.

Jenny had intended to wait for a few days until her father was properly rested before she tackled him about Aunt Clara's odd behaviour. But at lunch-time on Monday, after her lessons with Josh (who was up and about again), Mr Hanley arrived unexpectedly at Mariners Terrace.

"I would just like to have a few words in private with your father," he said.

Jenny ran upstairs to her room and remained there while the two men talked in the kitchen. Only when she heard Mr Hanley leave did she come back down.

Mr Lovett's eyes were shining as he turned to greet her. "It's such a relief to me to hear how well you're doing with Mr Hanley!" he exclaimed. "I was worried about your missing school. In fact – now I can admit it – I was worried about the whole set-up. About how you would settle down here. And how you would get on with Clara. But here you are! You've made friends. You're having private lessons. And you and Clara have hit it off famously. The next time I'm feeling really down, after a hard old stint hauling in those blasted nets, I'll think of that, Jen, and it will keep me going."

This little speech of her father's changed everything. For how could she possibly rob him of his peace of mind now, by asking questions about Aunt Clara? Or by letting him know that she was puzzled and worried by many things that had happened since he left? She simply could not do it. It would have been too cruel. So she kept quiet and tried not to feel too unhappy and apprehensive when, on 9 December, the evening before he left for Lowestoft, he sat at the table with her, pointing out, on the map of the British Isles in her atlas, the different fishing grounds he would be going to.

"We leave on 23 December for Plymouth, to go after the herring," he explained. "Then, at the end of January, we're off to Milford Haven, longlining for conger, ling and cod. Then off to Cardigan and Caernarvon Bay, working our way up gradually to the Shetlands for the herring in May."

"And then you'll come home?"

"Then I'll come home for a bit and see if I can find a place on a good racing yacht. That's where the money's to be made . . . You *are* happy at Clara's, aren't you?" he suddenly asked, as though a doubt had been nagging in his mind.

"Of course I am," said Jenny, smiling determinedly.

"The worst part of all is that he'll be away for Christmas," Jenny told Josh with a sigh, as they set off the following Monday afternoon with bags of grass-seed and fish-scraps for Godwit.

"So shall I," announced Josh gloomily. "We're going up to London to my sister Margot's on the nineteenth. She's hatching a baby apparently. Not that anyone's actually told me. But I heard Mother boasting to Mrs Buchan about it. And she can't move about much. So we've all to go to her. Like Mahomet and the mountain."

"Perhaps the baby will arrive while you're there," suggested Jenny, thinking it would cheer him up.

"I blooming well hope not!" Josh looked aghast.

"Why not? Don't you like babies?"

"I shouldn't think so. All that yowling! Anyway, I wanted to take bird pictures with my new camera," Josh pointed out. "I'd really been looking forward to doing that on Christmas morning after church."

"If the weather's like this, you won't miss much," said Jenny, pulling her tam-o'-shanter down over her ears.

It was a raw, foggy day, made eerie by the constant moaning of foghorns, and the track across the marsh to the Shepherd's House was soft with mud that clung to their boots and slowed them down. The only bird calls were the melancholy ones of invisible lapwings somewhere out on the marsh.

"Godwit will probably have gone upriver, reed-cutting," Josh remarked.

But he was wrong. The old man was standing at the grimy, cobwebbed window, obviously waiting for them. He opened the door as they walked up the path.

"Hoped you'd come," he said, smiling broadly. "I'm goin' to let owd Bottlebump free today. He's better now, an' he's pinin' for his home, I can tell. I'll need a bit of help, though."

"I should think you will!" exclaimed Josh as they followed Godwit into the room containing the cages. "How will you do it?"

There was a big hamper with an open lid standing in the middle of the floor.

"I'll have to bag him first. Then we'll put him in there. I want to take him up the river to the reed-bed where I found him," the old man explained.

Jenny watched nervously as Josh held the cage-door open and Godwit deftly enveloped the bittern in a sack. Then, between them, they gently lifted the struggling bird and dropped it into the hamper.

"It's all right. He has plenty of air," said Josh, seeing Jenny's look of concern when they fastened the hamper-lid. "Now for the boat-trip. Are you coming, Jen?"

"That's not very clean in the owd boat," Godwit warned her.

"You don't mind that, do you, Jenny?"

"Oh, no! I must see Bottlebump fly," cried Jenny.

Later, when she reflected on it, she thought it had been quite a hazardous journey. Even crossing the marsh to the jetty where Godwit's boat was moored was no easy feat in the fog. She had to hold on to the tail of Josh's coat as he followed Godwit and helped carry the hamper. Then there had been the trip upriver in the funny old flat-bottomed marsh-boat – which was so broad it seemed almost circular – with Josh punting and Godwit banging a frying-pan with a spoon every five minutes to warn other craft they were there.

But it had been worth it. Jenny knew she would always remember the freeing of the bittern: Josh lifting the hamper-lid, old Godwit whisking the sack from the bird like a conjuror and the two of them gently tipping the hamper over so that Bottlebump could walk out on to the gunwale.

"When he saw those reeds! The expression in his eyes!" she exulted later, walking home with Josh.

"And the way he took off," laughed Josh. "Did you see him? On those marvellous wings. Sailing straight across to his own special place in the middle of the reeds, I bet."

"And poor old Godwit calling, 'Good luck, owd mate, I shall miss you,' with the tears rolling down his cheeks. Poor old man! No one should be so alone."

"No." Josh's voice was sad. After a moment he said anxiously, "You won't forget him at Christmas, Jen, will you? That's his loneliest time of all."

"I won't forget him," Jenny promised. And, even as she spoke, an idea rolled into her head, making her miss her step and draw her breath in sharply, so that Josh turned round and asked politely, "All right?"

She nodded and smiled, but kept her lips tight shut, as though she were afraid the idea might come tumbling out too soon, before she had worked on it. By the time she reached home, she had decided it was to be a kind of Christmas gift for

Josh. One that would make his eyes shine and his cheeks flush with happiness. But she was going to keep it from him until the very last minute – the day when he would go off with his parents to London.

As Christmas approached, the north-westerlies and easterlies grew tired of Newbrigg. White, pinching frosts came in their place. When Jenny woke in the morning her breath smoked on the air and she was loathe to leave her warm cocoon to hop about shivering, teeth chattering, while she smashed the ice in her water-jug to wash. Pails of boiling water had to be carried continually along the rutted, iron-hard path to the lavatory, and Aunt Clara lived in dread of burst pipes.

Down on the beach, where the fish-boxes were piled high, the frosted pebbles glinted like precious stones and, when the auctioneer clapped two together to signify a sale, their ringing could be heard in the High Street.

Wood-smoke rose all day from Mr Block's fish-house, where hundreds of sprats hung from iron bars in the roof, and, by five o'clock every evening, the station-platform was piled high with boxes of dried sprats waiting to be loaded on to the London train.

"Mr Block's sprats is the finest in Newbrigg," Mrs Block told Jenny proudly.

Jenny guessed that he must be doing well, for Mrs Block had already bought the children their Christmas presents. She showed them to Jenny one morning when she went round for her cup of tea. New hoops for Charlie and Robert, a spinning-top for Samuel, a rag doll for Lizbeth, a knitted yellow duck for the baby and a pair of new kid gloves for Leila.

"What would be a suitable present for an old gentleman?" Jenny asked Mrs Block suddenly.

"An old gentleman? You don't mean yer dad?"

"Oh, no!" Jenny laughed. "I bought him two handkerchiefs as usual. I've put them in his duffle-bag . . . This is for a much older man."

"Do he smoke?" asked Mrs Block.

"I don't think so."

"What about peppermints? Old folk usually like them for their digestion."

"That's a good idea," agreed Jenny.

Her father had given her half a crown to buy her presents and she had already spent one-and-six of it on two handkerchiefs for him and one fancy, hand-embroidered one for Aunt Clara. She had a shilling left to buy presents for the Blocks, Josh and Godwit. In the end she decided to spend it all in Maggs' sweet shop, buying a quarter of mints for Godwit, a quarter of pear-drops – his favourite sweets – for Josh and a quarter of treacle toffee for the Blocks. It was the first time she could remember not having bought a Christmas present for Mrs Harris. If only their old housekeeper had written to tell them her address, she could at least have sent her a card, Jenny thought regretfully. The prospect of a Christmas without either Dad or Mrs Harris was not a very happy one. But it was made more cheerful by the idea she had thought up for making the twenty-fifth truly a day of goodwill.

When should she tell Aunt Clara of her plan, though? In the end she decided to wait until the Gales had left for London. What with all the Gales pre-Christmas entertaining and having to train the new housemaid, Ivy Glover (a pleasant but rather slow young woman, whose grandmother went to the chapel), Aunt Clara was having to work very hard up at Galaxy House.

"Are you sure you can't do more to help poor Clara?" Mrs Waspe hissed in Jenny's ear as they filed out of morning service on 18 December. "She looks worn to a shadow."

"She had to stay up late every evening last week, boiling the puddings for the Chapel Treat," Jenny pointed out – and had the satisfaction of seeing a guilty blush suffuse Mrs Waspe's face, for it was she who suggested Aunt Clara be responsible for the puddings.

Jenny knew that the Gales were leaving for the station at ten o'clock on the morning of the nineteenth, so she ran up to

Galaxy House a quarter of an hour before, just as the station-fly was rolling off with all the luggage and Jeremiah Double was backing Bess in between the shafts of the trap. Josh was standing alone on the gravel, outside the front door, a dreamy look in his eyes.

"I'm just wondering which camera Father will buy me," he told Jenny. "I wouldn't mind a Folding Pocket Kodak. Just to begin with, anyway. You can load them in daylight. And they're very easy to use."

"Here! I know it's early. But Happy Christmas!" said Jenny, shoving the bag of pear-drops into Josh's hand.

"Wonderful!" cried Josh. "My supply had just run out. And no one in London makes them like Miss Maggs. Here, Jenny, I have something for you, too." He drew a small, square cardboard-box from his jacket pocket and handed it to her. "You can open it now," he said encouragingly.

She pulled out a copper bracelet with the word 'Veritas' inscribed on it in large letters.

"Josh!" she gasped, turning pink with delight.

"Go on, Bluestocking! Translate!" he grinned.

"It means, 'Truth'," she said. "I only learned it last week."

"Do you like it?"

"I adore it! It's really beautiful. Only . . ."

"Only what?"

"It seems so much!" She looked unhappily at the small bag of pear-drops in Josh's hand.

"No, it's not," he said. "I can easily afford it. I had all my birthday-money still to spend. Besides, look at all you've done for me. Standing up to Father. Helping old Godwit."

It was the opening she had been waiting for.

"Josh," she said, watching his face intently, "I'm going to ask Aunt Clara if Godwit can spend Christmas Day with us."

"What?" Josh stiffened and his face straightened.

"I'm going to ask her tonight," she said. "I'm sure she'll say 'yes'. After all, it's what the Christmas story's all about, isn't it? That's what the preacher took for his text last Sunday. 'I was a

112

stranger and you took me in.' And, in a funny way, it will make up for Dad not being here."

Behind them, Mr and Mrs Gale had come out and were being helped into the trap by Jeremiah. Jenny could see Mrs Gale looking round for Josh.

Josh took a deep breath. "You mustn't do it, Jenny," he said. "It wouldn't work. You and I like Godwit. But to other people he's just a drunken old man."

Jenny glared at him. She felt so disappointed she could have burst into tears. "And I thought you would be so pleased!" she said bitterly.

"I'm sorry," said Josh. He turned red and bit his lip.

"But I'm going to do it – no matter what you say!" Jenny told him tightly. "As soon as you've gone, I'm going in to ask Aunt Clara."

"Don't!" cried Josh. He gripped her arm. "Please don't, Jenny! You'll upset Miss Lovett terribly."

"Come along, Josh! Hurry!" Mr Gale called impatiently from the trap.

"Upset her? Why?" Jenny stared at Josh coldly. She thought she knew why he was acting like this. It was plain, mean jealousy. He looked on Godwit as his private property. He did not want her trespassing when he was away. It was all right for her to trot along to see the old man for five minutes. But not to do any more.

"Your aunt doesn't like Godwit," Josh said lamely.

"Doesn't like him!" Jenny repeated scornfully as, in response to another shout from his father, Josh began to move reluctantly away. "I don't suppose she even knows he exists!"

"She does, then!"

"How do you know?"

"Everyone knows." Josh was walking backwards along the drive with Jenny following him. His face was scarlet. "Everyone knows," he suddenly burst out in a low, trembling voice, "because Godwit's your Aunt Clara's father. So there!" With a little gasp he turned and ran the few remaining yards to the trap.

Jenny stopped dead beside a big hydrangea bush, whose skeletal brown flower-heads rustled dryly in the slight breeze. She was still there, as though rooted to the spot, when the trap turned out through the front gates with Josh craning his neck anxiously to catch a last glimpse of her.

Chapter 13

So Godwit was Aunt Clara's father! In the days that followed Jenny could not stop thinking about it. At first it seemed incredible. But once she had recovered from the initial shock and had accepted the idea, she began to feel angry and scornful. For there was Aunt Clara, running around helping everyone with their Christmas preparations and being applauded on all sides, but pretending that her old, infirm father did not exist because he sometimes drank too much! And even if Godwit had once been such a great drunkard that the Lovetts had had to take Aunt Clara in (for Jenny decided that this must have been the case) he probably had been no worse than Mr Block, who had only given up strong drink because of his shipwreck.

Then, on the afternoon of the twenty-third, a Friday, Aunt Clara asked Jenny to take two baskets of sausage-rolls and mince-pies down to the Beach Company shed for the Old Men's Smoking Concert that evening, and, on the way, Jenny slipped a handful into her coat pocket for Godwit. After all, he's an old man, too, she thought angrily. He should surely be allowed to sample his daughter's baking. She would have been heavy-hearted anyway, for it was the day her father's boat sailed for Plymouth and she was trying desperately not to remember that, every minute, the distance between them was growing wider. But the weather made her feel even more melancholy. It was grey and bitterly cold, without a breath of wind, and the reeds and grasses stood up out of the hard-frozen ditches like ghostly spears. Occasionally some hungry bird cheeped plaintively, and halfway along the track to the Shepherd's House she almost stumbled over the pathetic little body of a skylark, its breast stained crimson by the bullet that had hit it.

Godwit was out (Jenny thought he was probably reed-cutting) so she left the sausage-rolls and mince-pies on his table upstairs where he would find them when he came in. Looking round the room, she was struck afresh by its misery and squalor. What a home for an elderly man to come back to after a hard day's work in freezing conditions like today's!

She was in no cheerier a frame of mind when she arrived back at Mariners Terrace. By then snowflakes were beginning to drift down.

"There you are!" said Aunt Clara good-humouredly, as she shoved a tray of biscuits into the oven. "Thought you'd got lost. What's the weather doin'?"

"Snowing," said Jenny listlessly.

"Is it?" said Aunt Clara. "Good job we didn't go up to Lowestoft then, like yer father suggested."

Jenny could not think what her aunt was talking about. "What do you mean?" she said.

"Oh, it was jest an idea yer father had. He thought I could maybe take you up to Lowestoft this mornin' to say farewell to him. You never say goodbye to a seaman. Did you know that? Superstitious lot! Not that Blowers is too bad, else he wouldn't be sailin' out on a Friday! Anyway, that's what yer father said. If I weren't too busy. But that would have bin whoolly a waste of a day. An' me with all this bakin' to git through!"

Jenny felt as though she were suffocating, as though her shock and rage and grief were great iron weights pressing down on her chest. She clung to the back of a chair and gasped, "But . . . but . . . ."

"It would only hev bin for half an hour anyway," said Aunt Clara as she dumped her mixing-bowls into the sink. "I thought it were some stoopid idea when he mentioned it. But I didn't like to say. Men never think there's work to be done."

Jenny gave a little moan. Then, bent over and with her arm pressed hard against her stomach as though she had a pain, she ran out of the house. She ran blindly, not knowing or caring where she was going, seeing nothing but the one picture in her mind's eye. Dad, watching and waiting on the quay at Lowestoft. Waiting and waiting, while hope gradually drained from his face.

When she finally stopped, exhausted, falling down on her knees on the shingle, she found that she had run far beyond the look-out tower to the lonely, bare stretch of shingle that Leila Block said was haunted. This was where the dead bodies were washed up. "Nine days down, and nine days up," Leila had whispered. In the gathering dusk the breakers pounding the beach became a giant stamping. Droplets of snow and foam flew in her face like arrows. It was a terrible place. Like the edge of the world, she thought. But the funny thing was, she was not afraid. As she knelt there all her fury and grief gradually drained out of her. She fingered the bracelet on her wrist, the one Josh had given her. "Veritas," she murmured. And a hard coldness slipped into her heart. When she finally rose to her feet and began to walk back along the sliding, rattling shingle, she knew that, for the first time in her life, she was deliberately going to try to hurt someone.

The house was empty when she walked in, the oil-lamp burning on the kitchen-table. She opened the top drawer of the dresser and took out a black pencil.

On the white wall, to the left of the range, she wrote in large letters, HONOUR THY FATHER. Then she sat down in the easy chair, her hands folded in her lap, and waited for Aunt Clara to return.

Jenny had had no clear idea of what would happen when Aunt Clara saw what she had done. She did not particularly care. Tears and shouting, to a greater or lesser extent, she thought, were probably inevitable. But she could not have foreseen what did happen. Aunt Clara stumbled in at the door with a cry of relief at seeing her there. She started to say, "Jenny! Where have you bin?" Then there was silence – a black, deep silence as though the floor had suddenly slid back and left them both crouching at the edge of a pit. Into the silence dripped the tick of the clock. Then, suddenly, steely fingers gripped Jenny's shoulders, hauled her out of her chair, across the kitchen, through the scullery and out into the yard. The door slammed shut. A key rasped in the lock. The kitchen window turned from gold to black.

She's locked me out! was Jenny's first incredulous thought. She hugged herself and felt the soft, fine wool of her dress beneath her palms. There was a covering of snow on the ground and the promise of more to come in the clouded night sky. Already she was shivering with cold.

She hammered furiously on the door. Again. And again. The house remained dark and silent.

"Aunt Clara!" she called, her voice cracking with self-pity. There was no answer.

It was only when she turned round, though, that she realized she was trapped. For the gate at the bottom of the garden, rarely used, was permanently locked and bolted. And the fences that divided Aunt Clara's garden from the Blocks' and Granny Fulcher's were six feet high.

She stumbled across to the Blocks' side. "Help! Help!" she yelled with all her strength.

There was no response. She guessed (rightly, as she found out later) that if they did hear her, they would mistake her shouts for sounds of revelry drifting along from the pub.

Already the cold was making her feel peculiar. Sick. And a little giddy. It was not helping, either, that she had had no tea. It was like some terrible nightmare. She found herself stupidly touching the ground to feel if it were solid. Then her eye fell on the shadowy hump that was the lavatory. It would provide some shelter at least. She made her way slowly along the hard path, stumbling over flints that were frozen to the earth. Then, stamping loudly, for it was daunting to go in there without a candle, she pushed open the wooden door.

117

"I must keep moving," she told herself, with vague memories of tales she had read about Arctic explorers.

She tried to remember the drill they had been given at Laurel Park: running on the spot, toe-touching, windmill-arms (this resulted in a set of grazed knuckles as she knocked her hand against the rough wall), but, after a little while, she felt herself slowing up. Her limbs and her brain both seemed to be stiffening. Before she quite realized it, she had stopped moving altogether and had sat down on the lavatory seat with her head against the wall. Her eyelids drooped.

Then, just in time, someone came into the Blocks' lavatory behind her. With a great effort of will she stood up on legs that felt like blocks of ice and banged drunkenly on the back wall.

"What's that?" called a shocked voice after a moment's dead silence.

"Mrs Block! Oh, Mrs Block! She's locked me out," Jenny moaned. Then her legs gave way and she slithered down the wall.

When she came to, she was swaddled in blankets and sitting in Mr Block's chair by the fire. Mr Block and Charlie had rescued her (as Charlie kept proudly pointing out) with the help of Mr Block's two ladders.

"Drink this, dear," said Mrs Block gently, holding a cup of warm, sweet tea to her lips.

She could feel the heat stealing back into her.

After a little while Mr Block lifted her wrist to feel her pulse. He nodded his head.

"She could probably drink another cup of tea by herself now," he told his wife. "An' you can loosen them blankets."

"But what happened to her?" demanded Lizbeth, coming forward.

"Yes. What happened to her?" echoed Samuel.

Mr and Mrs Block exchanged glances.

"Right," said Mr Block. "You three boys an' Lizbeth upstairs to bed! Early bed tonight. An' no grumblin'! Or Father Christmas might lose his way tomorrer!"

The children fled and Mrs Block sat down in her chair to change baby Lucy into her nightgown.

"Right, young Jenny," said Mr Block, perching on the end of the kitchen-table. "Tell us what happened then."

"You should never have done that, Jenny!" cried Mrs Block, aghast.

"Never!" said Bulldog harshly.

From being half-frozen to death, Jenny felt as though she were now going to burn up with shame. She must have made a poor job of explaining to them how she had felt that afternoon, she thought. Otherwise they would not be looking at her as though she were a criminal.

"But . . ." she began. Then gave up. What was the point? No one in Newbrigg was even going to try to understand her. For some reason they were all on Aunt Clara's side. But support came from an unexpected quarter.

"You can't blame Jenny," said Leila firmly. "She doesn't *know*."

Her mother and father stared at her, as though they were surprised at her even speaking. Then Mrs Block said, in a softer tone, "No. You're right, Leila. Of course she doesn't."

"What are we goin' to do now, though? That's the question," said Bulldog. "Should I go round and talk to her?"

"Yes. You go," said his wife. "But be careful what you say."

Mr Block went off, but he was back in five minutes. "'T'ain't no good," he said grimly. "She won't answer. An' the whole house is in darkness."

Mrs Block clasped the baby to her. "Oh, Bulldog!" she breathed. "You don't think she's . . ."

Jenny's head spun, so that she had to grip the arms of the chair.

"No, no!" said Mr Block impatiently. "But if she's taken one of her odd turns, she didn't ought to be left there on her own."

"Go and fetch Harriet Waspe," said Mrs Block suddenly. "If anyone can coax Clara out, she can."

Mr Block hurried off again. Leila shoved her chair close to Jenny, as though to show whose side she was on. Jenny smiled at her gratefully. Her world had suddenly become an ugly muddle. She felt that she needed a friend.

Twenty minutes later Mr Block walked in, followed by Mrs Waspe.

"She's come out. She's standin' outside at the gate," he told his wife.

"I'm taking her back home with me," said Mrs Waspe, coming forward and staring coldly at Jenny. Her pale face was streaked with tears. "She's suffered enough for one evening, poor dear. As for you, young lady," she finished bitingly, "I hope you're ashamed. Stirring up such trouble. And just before Christmas, too!"

Jenny had enough spirit left to defend herself.

"Why should I be ashamed?" she demanded shakily. "Because I think it's wrong for a poor old man to have to spend his winters in a bare, cold house on the marsh, instead of in comfort with his daughter?"

Mrs Waspe looked at Bulldog. "I think she must be told," she said, after a moment. "The sooner she learns the truth about her 'poor old man', the better for everyone. Perhaps you'll look after the girl," she called over her shoulder as she went out. "I'll keep Clara with us for Christmas."

"I *do* know the truth about Godwit," muttered Jenny, blinking back her tears.

"No, you don't, Jen," whispered Leila, looking at her sorrowfully.

"She wants to forget him," said Mrs Block, meaning Aunt Clara. "We all do. No one wants to remember Godwit Morley. Because of what he did."

"Twenty-five years ago," said Leila quietly. "That's a long time, Mam!" She had been patting the baby to sleep in her cot

120

in the corner. Now she had come back to her chair, and sat with her arms round her knees, gazing into the fire.

"It don't seem a long time. A terrible thing like that," said her father, looking at her reprovingly. "If you'd bin there when it happened, you'd understand."

Jenny felt as if a wind were chasing round inside her head. She pressed her hands against her temples as though to still it.

"What?" she asked urgently. "What?"

"You tell it, Liza," said Mr Block, drawing on his pipe.

"All right," sighed Mrs Block. She felt beneath her chair and drew out a piece of knitting. "But I'm warnin' you, young Jenny. It's not a pretty tale. It happened, as I said, twenty-five year ago . . . I were only seven . . . Bulldog was thirteen . . . It was on 23 September . . . ."

"1880?" Jenny sat up straight and gripped the arms of her chair. "The day of the boating accident?"

Mrs Block's knitting dropped in her lap, and Bulldog almost lost his pipe.

"You know about it?" Mrs Block said accusingly.

Their eyes, Leila's as well, had clouded. "If you've been leading us on . . ." they seemed to be saying.

"I know about the accident. That's all. Catchpole gave me a newspaper-cutting," Jenny told them.

"Ah!" Bulldog sighed for them all.

"Well, if you've read that, I don't need to tell you about the accident," Mrs Block said, her needles beginning to chatter again. "But what the newspaper didn't tell you was that those four poor souls might have bin saved."

"*Would* have bin saved," put in Mr Block, spitting into the fire, "if it had bin another man than Godwit Morley sittin' there."

"Oh, yes," said Mrs Block, her lips tightening, "he were there, Jenny. They could see him from the bank. Only yards away from those poor dears he were, all the time they were clingin' to that boat. But would he stir to help them? Not he! An' do you know fer why? The bird-stuffer had offered a sovereign for a spoonbill, an' Godwit Morley had seen one go

121

in the reeds. He were waitin' for it to come out, sittin' there in his owd punt. And as the last of them souls – Master Gerald it were – slipped into the water, Godwit Morley hit his spoonbill. Then he pulled it into his boat and paddled off down the river as fast as he could go!"

"An' jest after that Miss Annie's body come floatin' to the surface, her beautiful hair all spread out like seaweed," Bulldog put in in a hushed voice. "My father were in the first boat to arrive at the scene, an' they pulled the poor gel aboard an' tried to revive her. But that weren't no good. They'd to drag for the other bodies all that day an' the next."

"Lovely young people they was, too," said Mrs Block, her fingers slowing. "They did such a lot for the poor folk in the town. An' dear owd Miss Dora too, with her home-made medicines, and her soup-kitchen up at the house when times were hard. Many a time my mother went up there!"

"Miss Muriel was my Sunday-school teacher," said Bulldog with a reflective smile. "I thought there was no one like her."

"And everyone loved Master Gerald. A real little gentleman he were! An' so polite. Even to the likes of us. 'Oh, do forgive me,' he would say, if he bumped into you in the High Street. Quite like Master Josh he were."

Jenny rose unsteadily to her feet, her arms spread out like wings.

"Please," she gasped, "please . . . I think I'm going to be sick . . ."

Leila hauled her across the kitchen and shoved her into the scullery just in time.

Chapter 14

Jenny woke early the next morning when it was still dark. She lay peacefully for a moment before she remembered what had happened. Then she lit her candle and struggled out of bed, knocking against the wall several times as she made her way downstairs. She padded across the cold, dark kitchen and held the light high. Yes. There it was. The writing on the wall. The sight of it brought a wave of such nausea and dizziness that she had to sit down hard on the arm of the big fireside-chair.

Two hours later she stood at the door of Mr Hanley's lodgings, Number Twelve Back Street. Mrs Pipe, his fat landlady, looked at her askance.

"He ain't even had his breakfast!" she pointed out querulously.

Fortunately, though, Mr Hanley had overheard the exchange and he now appeared in the passage. "Problems, Jenny?" he asked anxiously.

When she nodded, he added, "I'll just fetch my coat and muffler and we can talk while we're walking. I'll be working up an appetite, Mrs Pipe," he called cheerfully as they left, "so you can start making that breakfast."

They turned down Vine Alley, crossed the High Street and walked the length of Vine Row to the promenade. There they walked backwards and forwards, like the fishermen did on Sunday mornings. The sea was like grey glass, the pebbles dusted with white frost.

"I knew about the old man, of course," Mr Hanley said sadly when Jenny had finished her tale. "I've often seen him on the river, taking his reeds up to Wenford. And then the older parishioners tend to talk about it when they're ill and depressed. It seems to have left a terrible scar. I suppose it's natural. I

123

mean the tragedy alone was bad enough. But you might have thought that, after twenty-five years . . ."

"He seems so gentle! So kind!" Jenny burst out. "I just can't imagine it."

"People change," said Mr Hanley, putting a hand on her shoulder. "That's why it's so wrong not to forgive. A sin, really. The vicar thinks the same. But feeling is so strong against Godwit Morley it would be useless even talking to them. They're a bit simple here. The local people, I mean. Like one of those Iron Age communities, I always think, shut inside a fort. In this case the ramparts are the North Sea and the river-walls. Besides, to resurrect the business would be bad for Miss Lovett. And then I often have the impression . . ." He stopped and gazed, frowning, out to sea, his hands in his pockets, shoulders hunched up.

"What?"

"I don't know . . . that there's more to it than I've heard. Something they wouldn't talk about to an outsider. Not even to their curate. Anyway," he added cheerfully, as they finally turned for home, "Miss Lovett will calm down when she thinks it over and realizes you acted mainly out of misguided compassion. She's a queer, highly strung lady. But she's not unreasonable."

"Should I write her a letter of apology?" Jenny asked.

"Yes. By all means. That should mollify her." Mr Hanley suddenly skipped aside to kick a stray flint against a lamp-standard as they crossed Chapel Street. "And don't worry about it, Jenny," he said. "The Waspes will look after her. And the Blocks will keep you right. They're good sorts . . . It's really all Josh Gale's fault," he finished, a shade peevishly. "He should never have introduced you to the old man in the first place."

"Oh, he didn't want to," said Jenny loyally. "It was just the way things happened. He had no choice."

"Well, don't let it spoil your Christmas," Mr Hanley told her firmly, as she left him at Mrs Pipe's door. "Next year at this time you'll wonder what you were worrying about."

124

Jenny ran off home, feeling much happier. She had been right to go to Mr Hanley. He always saw things in their proper perspective. When he talked in that slightly superior way about the people at Newbrigg being 'simple' and Aunt Clara a 'queer, highly strung lady', she felt she might be able to cope with them after all, and that what had happened was not completely her fault.

Once she had written a short note of apology to Aunt Clara, and had handed it (with Aunt Clara's Christmas handkerchief) to poker-faced Mrs Waspe in the shop, she found that she was quite enjoying the idea of spending Christmas with the Blocks. She helped Mrs Block and Lizbeth clean out the kitchen and polish the brasses in the morning. Then, in the afternoon, she went with Robert and Charlie to the plantation beside the golf-course, where they cut fir boughs and holly branches and pulled down long trailers of ivy to decorate the house. When they arrived back, she found that Mrs Waspe had brought round a letter from Aunt Clara. Her heart bumped a little as she opened it, but it was only a list of instructions about what food she had to take round to the Blocks and a reminder that her Christmas presents were in the sideboard in the parlour. She had not even added a note of forgiveness.

"Perhaps it's because she's tryin' to forget it ever happened," Mrs Block suggested, when Jenny pointed out this fact to her. "I reckon she's jest pretendin' to herself that she's bin feelin' poorly, an' that's why Harriet Waspe's lookin' after her. Her mind seems to work that way."

To help the illusion, obviously, Mr Block had gone round to Aunt Clara's that afternoon to whitewash over Jenny's offending text.

That evening Jenny saw Mr Waspe at the Children's Treat in the chapel, though neither his wife nor Aunt Clara were with him. She went over to him rather diffidently, after the game of Musical Chairs, to ask how her aunt was.

"Oh, coming along! Coming along nicely. You'll see her in chapel tomorrow, I expect," he said coolly, gazing at a point above Jenny's head.

Jenny did not relish this prospect. Indeed, every time she woke in the night – and since she had been invited to sleep at the Blocks' and was sandwiched between Leila and Lizbeth, this happened frequently – she felt queasy with foreboding. But in the end the encounter turned out quite differently from what she expected.

Aunt Clara, looking yellow and drawn, and leaning on Mrs Waspe's arm, came across to join Jenny and the Blocks at the end of the service.

"Happy Christmas! God bless!" she said warmly, shaking hands all round. Then her prominent brown eyes fixed on Jenny. "All right are you, Jenny?" she asked anxiously. "Find your presents?"

"Yes, thank you," said Jenny, her face crimson, since she felt that everyone must be blaming her for how Aunt Clara looked. "The Bible was lovely. It was just what I needed," she added, "and the Blocks gave me a hymn-book that matches."

"Your handkerchief was very acceptable too," said Aunt Clara, smiling wanly. "I have it with me." She opened her bag and pulled out the handkerchief, which trembled like an aspen leaf because her hand was shaking so badly.

"Come along now, Clara," said Mrs Waspe, as though she were talking to a child. "We'll go home and have dinner. Then you must rest again. We must have you fit for work on Wednesday."

As Jenny and the Blocks walked home, they passed gangs of rowdy young fishermen from the boats that had come home for Christmas and were anchored in the river. They stood on the corners, in their pointed boots and silk kerchiefs, shouting insults at their rivals. Mr Block smiled at them tolerantly, as though remembering his own young days, and Charlie cast envious glances at them. That evening, although it was Sunday, there was much drunken noise and singing in the streets, and Mr Block had to play his melodeon exceptionally loudly to drown it out.

The Block children, sleepy and full after the Christmas dinner of roast beef and plum pudding, and tired out with

126

chasing hoops, spinning tops and squabbling, were all in bed by eight o'clock. Baby Lucy slept soundly in her cot, clutching her duck; Leila sat at the table, painstakingly writing her thank-you notes to friends and relatives; Mr and Mrs Block dozed by the fire, and Jenny sat reading her new *Chatterbox* annual (the gift her father had left for her), and occasionally raising her eyes from its pages to wonder where her dad was at that exact moment, or to reflect guiltily on how ill and pathetic Aunt Clara had looked. The one person she determinedly steered her thoughts away from was old Godwit. She could not bear to think about him.

It was one o'clock on the Wednesday after Christmas and Jenny thought Josh was going to have a fit. He had come home from London in a foul mood anyway because of his Christmas present – which had turned out to be not a camera but a new dinghy, which was waiting for him in the Fields' boatyard. And now, when she had just confronted him with all she had learned about Godwit, his face had turned plum-coloured, and he had started to gasp like a fish. She was sitting in Mr Hanley's chair and Josh was standing on the other side of the big desk, his bunched fists pressed down on its edge, making eight little white knobs.

"You," he whispered with a choky sob. "You . . ."

"I know it's true," said Jenny coldly. "I've heard it from several different people. So you needn't try to deny it."

Josh's eyes bulged. "Heard what?" he said tersely. "Only their version of what happened. No one's ever wanted to hear Godwit's side. Not even you, Jenny Lovett! And you're supposed to be his friend. But you're just as hateful and vile as all the others!"

Jenny stared at him as though he were mad. "There couldn't ever be an excuse for what he did. Never!" she cried.

"Couldn't there?" said Josh tremulously. "Well, listen to this. No one else has listened in twenty-five years except me. To begin with, you don't even know why Godwit was so desperate to get that spoonbill, do you? Well, I'll tell you. His wife was dying of consumption. D-y-i-n-g. Understand, Jenny? The doctor said she needed special foods: chicken breasts, port wine. And do you know how much money Godwit had in the house when the doctor said that? Well, he didn't have much trouble counting it, I can tell you that! It was nil. Nothing. And then he had the little girl to keep alive. Clara. Her teacher said she was suffering from malnutrition. So when he saw that spoonbill flying into the reeds, he thought God had answered his prayers. He knew the bird-stuffer was offering a sovereign for a spoonbill, you see . . ."

"But that still doesn't . . ." Jenny started.

"Shut up," said Josh harshly. "I haven't finished. Godwit was waiting for the spoonbill to come out, when the *Shooting Star* went over. But he saw them all holding on to its side, and he kept thinking, Just another second and that bird will come out. Then I'll pick them up. Just another second. And he was so intent watching for the bird coming out that he didn't realize what was happening behind him. He didn't *realize*, Jenny! Just another second, he kept thinking. Then, when he had potted the spoonbill, he turned round and they were all gone. At first he thought they had been rescued. Then, when it dawned on him what had happened, he was so horrified he just shot away. Only he'd been seen from the bank. And when the story went round, all hell was let loose. He was hunted out of town, without being allowed to say a word in his own defence. And the really awful thing . . . the worst part of all . . . is that his wife had died while he was sitting in the punt waiting for the spoonbill."

A cinder plopped into the grate.

"That's the saddest story I've ever heard," said Jenny.

Josh's eyes kindled. "But you haven't heard the end of it yet," he said in a tight, angry voice. "They were ready enough to tell you what Godwit did. But they would never tell you what *they* did."

"They?" Jenny stared at him in bewilderment.

"All of them." Josh jerked his head in the direction of the town.

"What they did to Godwit?"

"What they did to Clara."

"But she was only a schoolgirl," said Jenny. "What age was she? Eleven?"

"Ten," said Josh. "That was what made it so terrible."

"But what could they do to her?"

Josh suddenly began to caper about the room, scratching his armpits and making grotesque faces. "This is what they did to her," he shouted. "Drove her screwy. Nuts. Ga-ga."

"Stop it!" cried Jenny, outraged. "Stop it this minute. You look disgusting."

Josh bumped down on the floor and sat hugging his knees and scowling at her. "It was them," he said sulkily. "*They* were the disgusting ones. Even talking about it infects you."

"But what did they do?"

"After Godwit went, Clara was put in the care of an old foster-mother who lived in one of those cottages opposite the drying-green. Then all the grumbling started. About the people in the town having to pay for her keep, after what her father had done. They said she should have gone with him. I suppose it grew worse and worse. Until one night some bright spark had the idea of organizing a Rough Band."

"What's that? A Rough Band?"

"It's what savages do when they want to drive people away," said Josh contemptuously. "They grab hold of anything they can make a din with. Pots and pans. Metal bars. Bird-scarers. Dustbin-lids. Norwegian horns. Then they stand outside the person's home and raise hell. There were hundreds of them that night. Children as well. Even though it was nearly midnight. It was Grandfather Gale who told me about it. He said he could hear the noise quite clearly from his bedroom."

Jenny almost felt as though she could hear it too. She had an urge to put her hands over her ears. "A girl of that age! She must have been terrified!" she cried.

129

"It was the old woman who was terrified," said Josh. "She threw Clara out into the middle of them. Just as she was, in a skimpy little nightgown, on a bitterly cold October night. But they didn't stop their hideous din even then. They kept on. And on. Until one of the clowns suddenly noticed the child was screaming, so Grandfather said. Then they all gradually fell silent. And there was this young girl, kneeling there in the middle of them, staring up at the sky, and making this terrible, high-pitched screaming sound."

Jenny felt herself begin to tremble all over.

"At that point someone had the sense to run for the doctor," Josh went on. "It was Doctor Buchan. Not our Doctor Buchan, of course. His father. He was the one who discovered that Clara couldn't see or hear any more. All she could do was make that horrible noise. So they carted her straight off to the lunatic asylum."

Jenny moaned, her eyes wide.

"Yes. It was pretty hideous," said Josh grimly. "And when the vicar and the schoolmaster heard what had happened, they made sure the whole town knew what a hideous thing they had done. Every week two parties were taken up to the asylum. One of schoolchildren and one of their parents. And they had all to file past the little room where Clara Morley was kept, sitting bound to a chair to stop her hurting herself. And every day in school they had to pray for her, and say, 'God forgive us for what we did to an innocent child.' And they said the same prayer every day in the church and in the chapel, until she was better. That wasn't until the following April. Then your grandmother said she would take her in. None of the Lovetts had taken part in the Rough Band, you'll be glad to hear. And that's why Miss Lovett is still a bit odd, to this day. And why they are all terrified of upsetting her. She's on their conscience still. And rightly too, don't you think so?"

But Jenny was lying across the desk with her head on her arms.

"Oh, poor Aunt Clara! Poor Aunt Clara!" she groaned. Then she began to cry. She cried and cried, her shoulders

130

heaving convulsively. And nothing Josh said could stop her anguish.

Chapter 15

Jenny could not stop feeling guilty about what she had done to Aunt Clara. Every time she looked at her and saw how she had aged, even growing more round-shouldered, since 23 December, she felt sick. She lost her appetite and could not concentrate on her lessons. Mr Hanley called her back on Friday, as she was about to follow Josh down to the kitchen for dinner.

"You're not still worrying about your aunt, I hope, Jenny?" he said sharply. "If you are, it's very foolish of you. She seems perfectly well again."

But Jenny felt that he would not have dismissed what she had done so lightly had he heard how little Clara Morley had once sat tied to a chair in the lunatic asylum. She was tempted to tell him, but could not in the end bring herself to do it. It was too painful a story.

Josh, too, noticed Jenny's depression. He said it was Catchpole's curse still working on them. "You look like the 'wretched wight, alone and palely loitering'," he told her as they tramped along to the North Marsh that same afternoon to feed the birds.

"Yes. That's just what I feel like," she said with a flat little laugh. " 'The sedge is withered from the lake and no birds sing'."

"They will soon, though," Josh said cheerfully as he began to scatter the soaked bread and the potato-skins along the edge of the footpath. "In another couple of months the redshanks will be whistling their heads off here. They sing all day and all night in the breeding season. Then, when the babies arrive, you can watch them scuttling along from their nests to the nearest pool for a swim. They look just like powder-puffs with matchstick-legs. If I had had a camera, I could have taken pictures of them . . . That was Catchpole again! Making Father give me a rotten dinghy for my Christmas."

"What I did was nothing to do with Catchpole," said Jenny tightly. "It was all my own work."

"But you're not makin' it any better, my love, walkin' round with that long face!" Mrs Block pointed out to Jenny when she met her on a Saturday morning in the High Street. "In fact you're makin' it worse. Clara's pretendin' it never happened. So you'll have to do the same, to make everything all right. Surely you realize that!"

Jenny felt as though the north wind that was driving everything before it along the High Street had suddenly swept through her brain. Of course Mrs Block was right! Why had she not seen it before? She must forget what had happened on the twenty-third – not because that was the easy way out, but to repair the damage she had done.

That afternoon, feeling happier, she went down to the chapel with the young Blocks, to help put up the decorations for the next day's Thanksgiving Service for the Harvest of the Sea. By then, the wind had reached gale force and, while they were draping the brown nets along the walls and hanging up the baskets, the lifeboat-guns went off. The three Block boys dashed out to the shed to watch the launch. But since the floats and all the flags from the local fishing-boats had still to be strung up, Jenny and Lizbeth carried on with their task. Jenny was glad they had done so when the boys returned an hour later, chilled and shaken, to report that three men had been lost from the stricken vessel (a ketch loaded with railway-iron) that had broken up on the sandbank. The passing-bell was already being tolled for them, and its mournful voice could be heard whenever the wind dropped.

Aunt Clara said scarcely a word that evening after she came home from work. Nor did she bring out her mending or her knitting, as she usually did. Instead she sat in the big fireside-chair, her fingers tap-tapping on its arm, and stared at the wall. When Jenny handed her her bedtime cup of cocoa and her toast, she started as though she had forgotten her niece was still there. And in the early hours of the morning, Jenny woke to hear her screaming again in a nightmare. This time she did not go to her aunt, but clapped her hands to her ears, until the screams subsided.

She hardly dared go downstairs on Sunday morning, afraid of what her reception might be. But in fact she found her aunt in the parlour, standing, serene and smiling, in the pale sunlight streaming through the window.

"Happy New Year, my mawther!" she called brightly, when she spied Jenny in the passage.

"Happy New Year, Aunt Clara!" Jenny replied in a voice wobbly with relief. And, for a little while, it really did seem as though they were going to have one.

The gales had died during the night and Sunday brought the severest frost they had had all winter. Every stretch of water was stone-hard and the young Blocks unearthed their skates from the alcove under the stairs.

"Though only fools will go out on the ice today," Mr Block said warningly, as they all walked home from the Harvest of the Sea service.

"Do you remember that chair Ted made one year, to push you round the ice, Clara?" Mrs Block asked suddenly.

"I certainly do, gel," replied Aunt Clara. "He pushed me that blinkin' fast across the mere we couldn't stop, an' we collided with a party of toffs from the Rectory. They went over like ninepins! I thought I'd have died of shame!"

Everyone laughed loudly, including Aunt Clara, and Jenny was aware of a feeling of sudden lightness, as though a heavy weight had just been lifted from her chest.

"You and I can go skating," Josh told her on Monday afternoon. "If this frost keeps up, the ice will be iron-hard by Wednesday, and we can go along the ditches near the

Shepherd's House then. No one else goes there."

"But I haven't a pair of skates," Jenny pointed out. "And I haven't enough money to buy any."

"Don't worry about that," Josh told her. "There's a box up in the nursery with hundreds of skates in it! There's bound to be some there to fit even your banana-feet! Let's go up and look."

True enough, Jenny soon found a pair with sharp blades and straps that looked hardly worn – they had been Margot's. She carried them home triumphantly at five o'clock to show Aunt Clara.

"Oh, yes! That's lovely for you," murmured her aunt, looking up absently from the letter she was reading. She nodded towards the table, where a second letter from the same envelope lay, still neatly folded. "From your dad," she said. "They've jest come by the afternoon post."

Jenny picked up the letter eagerly, for it was the first she had received from her father since he had left Lowestoft. It was dated Friday 30 December, and, to begin with, it was quite a cheerful account of how the crew of the *Good Hope* had spent Christmas. Mr Lovett thanked her for her handkerchiefs and described the Christmas Box of mince-pies, plum-puddings and small gifts that Bob Blowers' wife had made up for the men. But then he went on to say that they had been very disappointed in their catches. And, to make matters worse, on 28 December, a French boat had come so close to them that their nets had become entangled, so that they had been twenty-four hours hauling in, with nothing to show for it. Now they were all feeling very tired and rather dispirited, and thought they would move off westwards with the five other Lowestoft boats on Saturday morning.

"Poor Dad!" Jenny burst out. "What a rotten thing to happen!"

"Yes," sighed Aunt Clara, whose letter had obviously contained the same news. "That's a hard owd life an' no mistake!" Then she did something she had never done before. She walked across to Jenny, put her arm round her, and gave

134

her a squeeze. "Never mind," she said. "The months are passin', gel. Next thing you know, yer father'll be back home an' lookin' forward to havin' some fun racin'. He used to love racin', did Edward."

It was the kind of comforting remark that Mrs Harris, or Mrs Block, might have made. But to hear it from Aunt Clara was like receiving an unexpected gift.

Next morning, over their cup of tea, Mrs Block told Jenny how the town went mad when a big freeze came. The children played truant, the workers from the boatyard went without their dinner in order to skate on the marsh and, if the town smacks happened to be in the river, the younger fishermen became speed-fiends, skating along the ditches as fast as any motor-car.

Jenny had never skated in London, for Mrs Harris had not allowed her to venture on to the pond in their local park, where there was at least one fatality every winter. So she was keyed up with excitement, and found it very difficult to apply herself to learning the main dairy-farming districts of England and the 'quality of mercy' speech from *The Merchant of Venice*! Josh soon gave up any attempt to wrestle with his decimal fractions, and lay across his desk dreamily drawing little skating ducks all over the covers of his copy-book. For once, Mr Hanley did not nag. Perhaps he was infected with skating-fever himself. Because, as he took his leave of them at noon, he grinned and told them not to shake their brains up too much by falling about on the ice.

"I don't keep my brains in what we're likely to be falling on," Josh pointed out cheekily as they ran downstairs.

"Well, whatever you do," cried Aunt Clara, who had overheard him, "if you fall, lift yer hands up from the ice straightaway. Do you leave them there, you'll git yer fingers chopped off by some of them speed-skaters!"

"Not where we're going," Josh whispered to Jenny. "There will only be us there."

Because no one else wants to go near Godwit Morley, Jenny

135

thought, her smile dying. She had not been near him herself since before Christmas.

But then, as soon as she saw him that afternoon as he came hobbling along to watch them the moment he spied them on the ditch, she knew she could never dislike him. The Godwit Morley who had sat in a punt while four people drowned behind him was a hazy character in a story. She could not connect him in her mind with this soft-voiced, kind-eyed, raggedy old man who was trying to teach her to skate.

"Lean forward, my mawther!" he urged. "Forward! An' keep them feet at ten-to-two! That's it. Let yer knees bend. Now push. Push! Good gel. You're doin' fine . . . Whoops! Bump! Down she go!"

Gradually the bumps became less frequent. There were long, blissful minutes of gliding, when Jenny spread her arms wide and felt like a bird. Then came the triumph of skimming along the whole length of the black, gleaming ditch without once falling over. Josh, perfectly at home on the ice, skated in front of her, backwards, grinning and shaking the stiff white reeds and thistles that poked out from the banks, to sprinkle her coat with frost.

Neither of them wanted to stop. But at half-past three Godwit announced he had baked potatoes for them and was going in to make a pot of tea. It was only then, when Jenny clambered up on to the brittle, crackling grass to take off her skates, that she realized that her calves and her ankles were aching. It was a pleasant, satisfying ache, though. Part of a general feeling of content with herself and the world. The feeling persisted as she walked home along the track with Josh half an hour later.

"This has been one of the best afternoons of my life," she suddenly announced.

"Hear, hear! Mine, too," said Josh heartily. Then, for some reason, he looked furtively over his shoulder, as though he were afraid of being overheard.

"Who are you looking for? Catchpole?" Jenny asked teasingly, in a sepulchral whisper.

136

But later, when the smiles had been wiped from both their faces, she was to wonder if Josh had had a premonition of some kind. Had he feared that, by talking about their happiness, they might be tempting fate?

If so, he was soon to be proved right. It was a mere ten minutes later, when he arrived breathlessly at the North Marsh to leave some scraps for the coots, that he found a *For Sale* notice pinned to the post beside the track.

Twenty minutes after that Jenny opened Aunt Clara's front door to a weary-looking fisherman who said he was Jim Blowers, Bob Blowers' brother. He had come from Lowestoft to tell them that, on the previous Saturday, 31 December, there had been a terrible storm along the south coast. As far as was known, the *Good Hope* had taken shelter with five other Lowestoft boats in a small bay to the west of Plymouth. By evening the storm had grown to a hurricane and the bay was not sheltered enough to protect the boats. They had broken their moorings and been smashed to pieces. But although bodies and wreckage from the five other boats had been washed up, as yet none had been found from the *Good Hope*.

"So she may have survived and bin swept out to sea. They may still be alive," he finished, "though it seem a slim chance. But we jest don't know, missus. We can only hope an' pray."

"Hope an' pray," repeated Aunt Clara in a whisper. She had been about to put the kettle on the range when Jenny brought Jim Blowers into the kitchen. She was still holding it, as she leaned against the mantelshelf to steady herself. Jenny, who had sat down on her usual chair facing the dresser, was grimly clinging to the edge of the table, trying to ward off a faint. But it was no good. Icy water trickled down her spine. Her ears sang. With a barely audible moan she slid down on to the floor.

Chapter 16

Afterwards, when she looked back, Jenny realized that, once she had recovered from the initial shock of Jim Blowers' news, she had never for one moment really believed that her father had drowned. Or, to put it another way, she knew that he was still alive. Why? Perhaps she was helped a little by Mr Block's encouraging story of how he lay in a coma for two weeks after his shipwreck, so that no one in the hospital could find out who he was. Or by Leila's gripping her arm as they walked home from chapel and whispering, "I believe that faith can move mountains, Jenny. I really do! You have faith that yer dad'll come back, an' you'll see him again."

But mostly it was just a feeling that she had – like a warm cloak dropping round her shoulders whenever she thought of her father, and a certainty that he was somewhere, still thinking about her, still worrying about her, still planning out their future.

"Telepathy," Mr Hanley suggested, when she tried to explain this to him afterwards.

Whatever it was, it helped her through the worst times. When, for example, on the third Sunday after Jim Blowers brought his news, Mr Waspe pointedly asked the chapel congregation to pray, no longer for "the safe return of Edward Lovett", but for "our departed brethren, now safe with the Lord". Or when she woke in the night to hear Aunt Clara weeping in her bed, softly and heartbrokenly as though she would never stop. Or when Mr and Mrs Waspe came round, as they did more and more frequently, to sit talking with Aunt Clara in the parlour, in the low, hushed voices people use after a funeral.

So, although she wanted to know, with a constant, aching hunger, what had happened to her father, and where he was, she managed to carry on with her life. She felt happy when she was given her first Latin reader. She enjoyed baby Lucy's birthday tea. She managed to dissuade Josh from telling Mr Field that he wanted the name *Seasickness* painted on his dinghy and coaxed him into calling it *Roller* instead. She visited Godwit, went out with Josh on his mercy missions, and did her best to console him when the news about the North Marsh broke – the council was to sell it to one of three developers, all of whom had plans to drain it and build bungalows and hotels there.

"You know what will happen," Josh said in a tremulous voice. "The sale will go through just after the birds have nested and they'll start draining straightaway. They won't care."

"They might," said Jenny, but without much conviction, remembering Newbrigg's attitude towards birds.

"I don't know how you can even be bothered to think of such trivial things when you've jest lost yer father!" Aunt Clara burst out on the evening when Jenny told her how worried she and Josh were about the North Marsh.

It was 30 January, and, for several days now, Aunt Clara had hardly spoken, even at work, sitting preoccupied and silent at home, just as she had done on New Year's Eve. It was to try to break through her barrier of silence that, in desperation, Jenny had begun to talk about the North Marsh. Now, when her aunt turned on her, she cried indignantly, "But I don't believe Dad is dead! I just know that he's not!"

"Oh, gel!" said Aunt Clara with a little moan, "You're only makin' it harder on yerself. Accept it. Why do you think we've not heard from them, if they're not all gone? It's a month since yer father wrote his last letter."

"But nothing's been found. No wreckage," Jenny said stubbornly.

"The sea don't make deliveries to order," Aunt Clara said, standing up. She was holding on to the arms of her chair and trembling like a leaf. "If it want you, it'll take you without leavin' a trace. It's had three from this house now."

"I didn't argue with her any more," Jenny told Mrs Block

over her cup of tea next morning. "I thought that was best."

"Yes, my darlin'. That's right," said Mrs Block in an oddly thick voice.

Soon after this, Jenny became aware of people going out of their way to be kind to her. Mr Gale invited her to accompany him and Josh on *Roller*'s first short trip to Decoy Point and back, and was very kind to her, telling her she would make a first-class sailor. Old Mr Gocher staggered round one evening with a model of the Blackrock Lightship for her, which he had carved when he still had a steady hand. Charlie and Robert Block hunted for amber and jet for her on the beach. Even Mrs Waspe brought her sherbert and liquorice from the shop, when she came round to see Aunt Clara.

"Josh! You don't believe that my father's dead. Do you?" Jenny asked, coming to a sudden halt one afternoon as they were battling, against the wind, along the track to Godwit's.

"I wouldn't dare to," Josh replied, grinning at her fierce scowl. Then his face became serious. "I believe what you believe," he said. "I believe in you. There!" And he leaned over and kissed her awkwardly on the cheek.

Jenny's face was still burning when they walked in on Godwit and found him sitting on an upturned crate, surrounded by his birds, and with his fist pressed against his chest.

"Blast!" he greeted them. "I fare to git some indigestion-attacks these days. I could be doin' with some more of them peppermints you brought me las' time, young Jenny."

"You ought to drink hot water," Jenny told him, looking in vain for the kettle on the range.

"Ain't bin to the owd pump yet," the old man said between clenched teeth.

"I'll go," cried Josh.

The pump was just outside, beneath the kitchen window. Josh was back in a couple of minutes with the filled kettle, which he sat on the boiler of the range. By the time the water was heated, though, Godwit's face was quite grey. And it was another half-hour before he was comfortable enough to show them the latest additions to his hospital – a curlew with a broken wing and a coot that had almost died of starvation.

"I expect it's his drinking that's giving him indigestion," Josh remarked to Jenny on the way home.

"Yes," said Jenny slowly. "But perhaps if he didn't drink, he would have a worse kind of pain. I mean . . ." But then she could not find the words to explain what she did mean.

Josh was only half-listening. He had been staring towards the river. Now he let out a cry. "The town smacks! They're beginning to gather for the Westward mackerel-voyage. Let's run to the end of the quay and have a proper look at them."

There were about a dozen smacks rocking gently in mid-channel with gulls wheeling and mewing around them. Small boats were plying to and fro between them and the quayside.

"They're taking their stores on board," Josh explained. "There's Lucky Fulcher's *Omar* just opposite us. Do you see?"

But, suddenly, as often happened nowadays, Jenny lost all interest in what was going on around her. Her longing to see her father, which was with her all the time like a nagging toothache, suddenly became so overwhelming that she could think of nothing else. She walked home by Josh's side, struggling to hold back her tears, grateful for his sympathetic silence.

Two nights later, she woke to hear what she thought were people talking on the staircase. Wondering whether someone had called late with news of her father, she leaped out of bed, groped her way to the door, and pulled it open. Immediately she realized her mistake. There was only one voice, that of Aunt Clara saying her prayers loudly and fervently. Jenny quickly shut her door again. But not before she had heard her aunt ask the Lord to help her decide what was to be done with 'Edward's gel'.

To be done with me! thought Jenny, feeling quite shaken as she climbed back into bed. There was an ominous ring to that phrase. She sat up in the dark, hugging her knees and listening to the low roar of the sea and the louder booming of the wind across the marshes. Being so certain that her father was still alive (and at that moment she felt it more strongly than ever) she had never paused to consider that Aunt Clara was viewing the situation through different eyes. To her, Jenny was now an orphan, whose future had to be mapped out.

But, after a few minutes' hard thinking, Jenny's panic subsided. Aunt Clara was not likely to offend Mrs Gale by depriving Josh of Jenny's company. So she must be worrying about what to do with her when Josh returned to school in September. By which time, of course, she and Dad ought to be back in London!

Anyway, she told herself, a letter was bound to come from Dad soon. Wherever he was – in hospital, stranded on the coast of France or Spain, on some ocean-going ship that had rescued him – he must eventually be able to contact them. Until then, it was just a question of trying to keep Aunt Clara as calm and as free from anxiety as possible.

For a week boisterous weather had kept the town smacks tossing fretfully in the river, unable to leave for Newlyn, where, if the *Eastern Gazette* were to be believed, the East Anglian boats, already there, were making heavy catches. The crews wandered about disconsolately between the Beach Company shed and the quay, watching the weather in the hope that there might be a sudden change for the better.

"Poor lads," Mrs Block remarked to Jenny. "They can't even go eel-pritchin' or wild-fowlin' to git a bit of money. For if the wind drop sudden-like, an' the tide's right, they'll be off. An' they've no money for beer, so they can't go in the pubs. No wonder their faces is longer than owd Waspe's sermons!"

Jenny was wishing the smacks on their way for her own reasons. Bulldog had told her that every one of the twenty crews would be trying to find out what had happened to the *Good Hope*, and that any news would be sent home straight-away to Aunt Clara. So her heart lifted when, on that Thurs-day – calm and sunny at last – she found the baker's crowded with cheeky, jostling smacks' boys, collecting their bread. She waited on the pavement outside until the last of them had hurtled by her and gone tearing along to the quay as fast as his loaded basket would allow.

"They're ready to sail . . ." Leila began as Jenny walked in. Then her hand flew to her mouth and she gave a gasp of dismay. She pointed to three loaves sitting on the trolley beneath the side window. "Oh, dear! Those were for the *Omar*," she whispered, looking fearfully over her shoulder, as though she were afraid Mr Ball might hear her from the bakery. "Mr Ball brought them through after the others, and I've forgot to put them in the basket . . . Oh, Jen! He's in such a bad mood today, too, 'cos his chest's poorly!" Her sallow face had turned pink and she was biting her lip, as though she might burst into tears at any moment.

"Quick! Put them in my basket," Jenny told her. "I'll run along to the quay and catch the boy."

"Oh, thanks, Jen! Thank you!" Leila's gratitude was pathetic. A timid, conscientious soul, she lived in fear of losing her job, as Jenny knew.

Jenny was a fast runner but, even so, by the time she reached the quay, every boy was already sculling his boat, with its cargo of bread, across the water. Indeed, the *Omar*'s boy had almost reached his smack. Without hesitation she ran to the side of the quay, where the Gales' rowing-boat was moored, and climbed down into it. Thanks to Josh's tuition, she was perfectly at home in it now, and she was soon rowing, with strong, smooth strokes, towards Fulcher's smack. All around her, brown sails were being hoisted and anchors hove up, the wheeling gulls screaming an excited accompaniment to the rattling chains, the groaning ropes and the shouts of command from the various skippers.

Drawing alongside the stern of the *Omar*, Jenny shipped her oars and grabbed hold of a rope that dangled over the smack's side. Then she stood up and gave a loud hail.

The tow-haired boy appeared first, gaping stupidly down at her as she explained about the three loaves.

"Here! Catch!" she cried impatiently, tossing them up to him, one by one.

Then, as the boy, still dumb and round-eyed, caught the last one, a voice roared in Jenny's ears and she looked up into Lucky Fulcher's purple face. The next moment, her hand was knocked roughly from the rope and she sat down with such a bump that the rowing-boat almost went over.

"And if you had heard his language!" Jenny told Josh shortly afterwards in the schoolroom. "I had to put my hands over my ears first. Then I had to row away as fast as I could. It was shocking!"

"It would be!" said Josh, his eyes large with dismay. "A female person touching Fulcher's *Omar*!"

"But I was doing him a good turn!" Jenny pointed out, her face pink with temper. "If I hadn't taken them their stupid bread, they would have run out before they reached Newlyn. So how dare he swear at me!"

"I told you before," said Josh, "he takes after that old witch, his mother. There's no reasoning with them. They're superstitious, with a capital S. I don't want to worry you, Jenny," he added in a low voice, as Mr Hanley loomed in the doorway, "but I have a nasty feeling that you haven't heard the end of this."

"Your prophetic soul again!" Jenny said to him shakily that afternoon, as they stood staring at each other in Aunt Clara's kitchen, after Mrs Block had waylaid them with her bad news.

"Well, I was pretty sure Lucky wouldn't sail today, after what happened," Josh began.

"After *I* happened, you mean," Jenny put in bitterly.

The boy nodded solemnly. "And tomorrow is Friday, so he won't sail out then. And if they do leave on Saturday, they'll have to lay up somewhere for Sunday. So they're going to be about five days behind the other smacks in reaching Newlyn, and they'll lose all that money. It stands to reason that the crew must feel upset. Still . . . I never thought they would have done that!"

What the crew had done was to come marching up in an

144

angry body, with their wives and children, to Mariners Terrace, to tell Miss Lovett what they thought of her stupid niece. ("An' Lucky an' Granny Fulcher standin' at their gate, eggin' them on!" Mrs Block had said disgustedly.)

Aunt Clara must have seen them, as she came hurrying down Wall Road from work at quarter-past two, and she had such a fright, that, before any of the crowd had a chance to say a word, she burst into hysterical weeping and went flying by them, along the High Street to her friends, the Waspes. Harriet Waspe had arrived on the scene a few minutes later, demanding to know what was afoot. "An' when they told her, didn't she give them a piece of her mind fer upsettin' Clara!" said Mrs Block gleefully. "Even owd Granny Fulcher slunk away indoors."

"And I bet she's giving me a piece of her mind right now," Jenny said grimly to Josh. "I just know what she'll be calling me! 'Burden.' 'Troublemaker.' 'Pain in the neck.' "

"Never mind! It's sticks and stones that break your bones," said Josh cheerfully, as he took her elbow and steered her towards the door. (They had been on their way to the river, when Mrs Block's news had diverted them.) "You shouldn't ever worry about what people *say*, Jenny Wren!"

But, in this instance, it turned out that Jenny had every reason to worry. For what the Waspes were saying about her to Aunt Clara at that moment was to affect the whole course of her life.

Chapter 17

It was as though everything conspired that following week to blind Jenny to what was going on. There was so much to distract her. There was the excitement of her first East Anglian Valentine's Day with a gift left for her on the doorstep in the morning – a packet of 'Five Boys' chocolate from Aunt Clara.

There was Mr Hanley's startling suggestion that Josh should draw up a petition to save the North Marsh and ask local naturalists to sign it. Godwit had a drinking-bout that lasted for three days. And Mrs Block had a surprise encounter in Ipswich with a happy-looking Catchpole, who told her she wished she had moved years before, for she now had a job in a hotel with better wages, fewer hours and plenty of company.

"I expect she's lifted her curse then," said Josh, so seriously that Jenny shook her head at him.

"You didn't really believe in that curse, I hope," she said scornfully. "If you did, you're as bad as Lucky Fulcher."

Still, she felt relieved about Catchpole. For no matter how unpleasant the housemaid had been, she would have hated to think of her starving, or in the workhouse.

Most misleading of all, though, was the change in Aunt Clara. A change for the better, Jenny naturally thought. For although her aunt was still quiet, a glance at her face showed that her poor brain was no longer churning with worries and fears. She looked a little tired, but quite calm.

Yet, if Jenny had paused to consider, there were clear indications that something unusual was afoot. For almost every evening her aunt was closeted with the Waspes in the parlour, and, when Jenny passed the door, she could hear papers rustling and low, solemn conversation. Then, on 24 February, Aunt Clara took a day's leave, with Mrs Gale's permission, to travel up to London with Mrs Waspe. "To attend to some family business," she explained briefly to Jenny.

"It must be important business for Aunt Clara to leave Ivy Glover in charge of her precious kitchen. She never stops grumbling about how slow she is," Jenny commented to Josh.

How important the business was Jenny discovered the following Sunday evening. She was about to make her cocoa at nine o'clock, when Aunt Clara called to her from the parlour doorway.

"Harriet an' Amos have suffin' to say to you, gel," she said, pushing Jenny in to the front room. "I'll be through in the

146

kitchen makin' the supper." She looked happy and excited, and sounded slightly breathless.

Mr and Mrs Waspe both rose from the sofa as Jenny came in. What were they going to lecture her about this evening? she wondered. Or were they going to ask her again to help with the Sunday School?

"Sit you down, child," said Mr Waspe solemnly, nodding towards the place he had just relinquished on the sofa. He clasped his hands behind his back and rocked thoughtfully on his heels.

Jenny felt a prickling of unease. Both the Waspes looked extraordinarily serious. She sat down warily, watching Mrs Waspe fiddle with the cameo brooch which she always wore at the neck of her drab woollen dresses. Suddenly the woman sat down beside her and gripped her hand.

"Well, Jenny," she said, taking a deep breath, and smiling determinedly, "we have some good news for you. You are a lucky girl. Isn't she, Amos?"

Mr Waspe nodded silently and fixed his eyes on the corner of the ceiling.

"Why am I lucky?" For some reason a shiver ran down Jenny's spine.

"Well, because you have been given a place on Mr Bright-way's Emigration Scheme, my dear." Mrs Waspe's voice was as soft as plush. "Yes, indeed. You are going off on a great adventure. To Canada. To live in Toronto, which is a most beautiful city, with the Reverend Colin McDonald and his wife. You will help with the children, which you are bound to enjoy. We went to a great deal of trouble to find a suitable place for you. There is the chance, too, that you may be able to continue with your schooling part-time."

Jenny felt numb. Was it a bad dream? She could not believe this was happening to her. It was like the night when Aunt Clara had locked her out. Her palms were suddenly cold with sweat. Her teeth began to chatter.

Then Mr Waspe suddenly bent over her, his hands on his knees, and stared at her over his spectacles. "Well?" he said sharply. "What do you say, Jenny Lovett? We have gone to a great deal of trouble on your behalf. Are you not forgetting your manners?"

Immediately Jenny's courage flooded back. She stopped shivering. "Going to Canada!" she cried in an outraged voice. She glared from one to the other. "You must be mad! I'm not going to Canada. If my father could hear what you've just said . . ."

She saw Mr Waspe's face crumple with displeasure, before he straightened and turned away. Then Mrs Waspe took her by the shoulders and swung her round to face her. Her smile had vanished. Her pale eyes gleamed angrily.

"Now, listen to me, young lady!" she said tightly. "You are not an infant. It is time you faced facts. Your father has been drowned these two months . . ."

As Jenny opened her mouth to refute this, Mrs Waspe's fingers tightened and she went on hurriedly, "We are extremely sorry about it, of course. We did not know Edward Lovett personally, but we have heard only good of him. However, Jenny, life must go on. And not just your life. Clara's life, too. That is what has been causing us grave concern. Your Aunt Clara's life has been a very troubled one. She was younger than you when . . ."

"I know all that," Jenny broke in resentfully. She wriggled out of Mrs Waspe's grip and shuffled along the sofa, so that she was as far away from her as possible.

"Well, if you knew it, you should have been a sight more considerate," Mr Waspe called snappily from the fireside-chair where he was now sitting.

"She doesn't know anything! You don't know anything, child!" cried Mrs Waspe, pulling at her brooch again. "That poor, dear soul! Such a childhood as she had! Then losing Mr Lovett and Alfred so cruelly. And having to nurse old Mrs Lovett while carrying on with her job at Galaxy House. Her nerves were at breaking-point many a time. Then, just when it seemed she was to have some peace at last after all her trials, your father's letter arrived . . . We were furious! We won't pretend otherwise . . . But Clara insisted it was her Christian duty – and I suppose it was – to help him and take you in. But it seems our worst fears have been realized, haven't they, Amos?"

Mr Waspe grunted.

"Our *worst* fears," Mrs Waspe said emphatically. "Clara is not strong enough to cope with you, my dear. That's the crux of the matter. It was worry enough for her when your father was alive – look how you upset her before Christmas! – but since she has been carrying the burden of responsibility on her own . . ."

"She has been falling apart," Mr Waspe broke in. "That business with Fulcher and his men, it was the last straw. As Clara's friends, we could not allow it to go on."

"This is the best solution for you both," Mrs Waspe said, reverting to her soft, persuasive tone again. "You will be grateful to us one day, my dear. Canada is the land of golden opportunity for such as you, life's little unfortunates. You will be leaving in two weeks' time," she went on more briskly. "Dear Mr Brightway is waiving the usual formality of a medical certificate, because we can vouch for you."

Jenny, pressing herself in to the corner of the sofa, was struggling to breathe. Trying desperately to dredge up breath that would not come. Then, just as she felt she was surely going to suffocate, Aunt Clara walked in with the supper tray.

Jenny sprang to her feet, flew out of the open door, up the stairs and into her room. She staggered across it, tripping over a stray shoe in the dark, and dropped on her knees beside her father's trunk. Opening the lid, she pulled out the jacket of his best suit and held it tightly against her chest.

"Dad!" she gasped. "Oh, Dad! Where are you?"

Then she began to weep, with deep, groaning sobs, as though her heart were being tugged slowly from her body.

"You are not going," said Josh.

It was Friday afternoon. Five days had passed since Jenny had

149

learned of the plan to send her to Canada. She was sitting with Josh on a bollard at the end of the quay. It was the same bollard she had sat on that long-ago afternoon when her father had brought her here for the first time. If she shut her eyes, it was now as though he were standing just behind her. Warm. Caring. Alive. She *knew* he was alive. She knew! But how to convince people? Only Josh believed her – loyal, fierce little Josh.

"You are not going!" he muttered again.

The tide was out. Jenny stared bleakly down at the mud, where a black-headed gull hopped awkwardly, trailing a wounded leg behind it. He would not last long, she reflected. Not unless Godwit caught him. The other birds would mob him when he grew weak through lack of food. Nature was very cruel. Life was very cruel.

She had to go to Canada. No one could stop it happening. Her friends had tried. Mr Block had gone up to Lowestoft, in the vain hope that something more might have been heard of the *Good Hope*. Mr Hanley had twice gone to remonstrate with the Waspes, but without results. Even Mrs Gale, before she went off to London for her daughter's confinement, had taken time to go into the kitchen to ask Aunt Clara if she was sure it was the right decision. Aunt Clara had replied that she was quite sure.

Aunt Clara was Jenny's legal guardian. She had a paper, signed by Jenny's father, to prove it. And now that she had signed another paper, saying that she wanted Mr Brightway to take Jenny to Canada, there was nothing anyone could do to prevent that happening. Apparently, Mr Brightway could even send children to Canada without notifying the parent or guardian who had put them in his Home. Mr Hanley said this was a scandal. He said that people like Mr Brightway started out by doing good, but ended up trying to play God. He said that a question ought to be asked in Parliament.

But Aunt Clara thought that Mr Brightway was a saint, and that Canada was a kind of paradise. She said that Jenny would be 'a brick to build the Empire' and she could not stop talking

150

about what a fine family the McDonalds were, and how happy Jenny would be with them. She was knitting Jenny warm stockings and gloves, and making her new underwear to take to Canada with her. She was so relieved at the thought of Jenny's going, that every evening she sang while she worked, tapping her foot jauntily on the oilcloth. And Jenny suspected that even people who had been shocked in the beginning by the idea of Jenny's being sent to Canada – people like the Blocks – were now coming round to Aunt Clara's point of view, because they saw how well and happy she was looking.

"Oh, Josh!" Jenny crumpled suddenly, unable to bear up a moment longer. She fell against him, gasping and shuddering. "I'm so frightened! I don't want to go to Canada. I don't want to leave everyone I know. Dad might never find me again!"

"Jenny!" Josh put his arm round her and pulled her back roughly, so that she had to look into his face. His eyes blazed at her. "Didn't you hear me? I said you are not going!"

"But . . . how?" she asked, a sob choking her.

"That's what I'm trying to work out," he said impatiently. "You must run away from here. I know that much. The question is where to. Is there anyone in London who would hide you?"

She pulled herself together and tried to think. After a minute she shook her head desolately. Even had she been writing to Mary Moore regularly, Mary's parents were not the kind to want to harbour a runaway. Nor was Miss Grant.

"No one?" Josh's face puckered in dismay.

"There is one person –" she was thinking of Mrs Harris, who, she knew, would stand between her and an army of Brightways, if necessary "– but not in London. In Glasgow somewhere . . . but I don't know where. She hasn't written again. She was moving. Mrs Harris – our old housekeeper. Wait a minute!"

She felt beneath her coat and, from her dress pocket, pulled out the envelope which contained her most precious letters. She found the one Mrs Harris had written before Mr Lovett's birthday, and spread it out on her knee for Josh to read.

"Oh, look! On the south side. Overlooking a park," he cried

excitedly, after studying the letter for a minute. "There can't be all that many parks on the south side of Glasgow. What you must do is ask a policeman for directions, once you arrive there. Pretend that you're going to Mrs Harris's about a job, and that you've lost the address. You do look old enough to be travelling about on your own. That's a blessing."

Jenny stared at him. "Josh, you're mad!" she exclaimed finally, her voice breaking. "How can I possibly go to Glasgow? I have only threepence in the world."

"That's no problem," he said, with a long-suffering sigh. "I'm not a complete fool. I have money. Mother keeps it for me in a box in her room. But I know where the key is. I haven't touched any of my Christmas money. So I must have almost three pounds. That should take you to Glasgow."

"I can't use your money!" protested Jenny. "You're saving up for your camera and all your photographic equipment. I know you are."

"Your staying in this country means far more to me than a camera," Josh said sternly. "In fact I feel rather insulted that you should think it might not."

"Oh, I don't know what I think!" cried Jenny, clapping her hands to her head. "My brain just goes round and round. I've hardly slept since they told me."

"All right, old thing! Calm down," said Josh, patting her on the shoulder. "I'll do the thinking for you. We know where you are going now, at any rate. And money is no problem. So . . ."

"But, Josh!" Jenny broke in distractedly. "Mrs Harris might not even be in Glasgow. How do I know? What if I go all that way and can't find her?"

Josh leaned forward. "Look, Jenny Lovett!" he said fiercely. "If you sit here waiting for a miracle, you'll be in Toronto next month at this time. So you had jolly well better go to Glasgow and hope for the best. If, by any slim chance, you don't find your friend, Mrs Harris, you'll have to give yourself up to the police and be brought back. But at least you will have tried."

Looking at Josh's set, stubborn face, and hearing the determination in his voice, Jenny suddenly realized that here was a will stronger than her own. Probably stronger than Mr Block's or Mr Hanley's. Stronger even than his domineering father's. It had grown steel-hard in his long battle to be himself.

"All right, Josh. I'll do whatever you say," she said meekly.

"Good." Josh's mind was already running on ahead. "I'll have to find a railway-timetable," he muttered. "Then we must think how to put them off the scent. It's a long journey to Glasgow. We don't want them coming after you on the train." He slipped down from the bollard. "I'm going for a walk, Jen," he said abruptly. "I can think better on my own. I'll meet you tomorrow morning at eleven by the look-out tower, and tell you what I have decided."

She watched him walking off along the quay. A skinny little boy with his hands dug into his pockets, and his shoulders hunched. A skinny little boy, upon whom her whole happiness depended.

Chapter 18

The arrangement was that Aunt Clara and the Waspes would escort Jenny to the Brightway Home on the following Saturday, 11 March, so that she could set off for Liverpool with the other emigrating children on the thirteenth.

"So we will make our plans for Wednesday," said Josh in his new, authoritative voice. "Then, if the weather's unkind, we have two days in hand."

They were standing with their backs against the look-out tower, facing a blue, white-frilled sea.

"What has the weather to do with it?" Jenny asked timidly. She felt like a private soldier cross-questioning a general.

"You can't leave from Newbrigg station," Josh told her. "They would be bound to remember you. But Wenford's a junction. It's much busier. No one will give you a second glance there. I shall take you there in *Roller*."

153

"Oh, Josh!" said Jenny, her voice trembling.

"It's all right," said Josh, giving her an amused look. "I have done it before. Every Gale has to be able to sail a dinghy, single-handed, to Wenford and back. Even Margot managed it once. On Tuesday evening, while your aunt is still up at our house, I'll bring down one of the old Gladstone bags from the luggage-room in the attic. You can pack what you'll need in that, and I'll take it down to the river and stow it in *Roller*. No one will suspect anything, even if they do see me. They'll think I'm just stowing away gear for my own use."

"But won't I be spotted with you in the boat on Wednesday?"

"Not if you squat down in the bottom of her," Josh said. "I'll have her ready at Field's landing-stage at nine o'clock in the morning. You must come to the boatyard between the two sheds, keeping your head well down, so that you're not seen through the windows. The men stop for breakfast then, so they will all be inside."

"What about Mr Hanley? What will he say, when you don't turn up for lessons?" Jenny's own schoolroom days were over, for Aunt Clara thought she should use the time remaining to her to help wash, iron, and mend the clothes she was to take to Canada.

"I'm to have a week's holiday," said Josh with a faint smile. "I told Father I couldn't wait to try *Roller* out, and Mother's not here to object."

Although she was wearing her thick coat, Jenny was shivering with nerves.

"How long will it take us to sail to Wenford?" she asked.

"I don't know," Josh admitted. "It all depends on the weather. But the best train for you to catch would be the four-thirty. We should make that quite easily. It arrives in Liverpool Street at seven-thirty, and the night-train for Glasgow leaves Euston at ten. I've written it all down for you. You should be safely in Glasgow by seven next morning. You might even be able to afford a sleeping-berth, if there's one vacant. You *will* be all right, won't you?" He looked at her dubiously.

"I think so," she said, biting her lip.

"I would have come with you," he went on. "Only I don't expect your Mrs Harris would have wanted to hide me as well. Besides, I must keep my eye on Godwit. He hasn't looked well since that last drinking-bout. And I have to find more signatures for the North Marsh petition. You know how important that is."

"Yes, I do," said Jenny shakily. "I just wish I could have been here to help you. It's when I talk about leaving, that I realize how much I'm going to miss Newbrigg. How much I'm going to miss the Blocks, and Mr Hanley and Godwit. But you most of all, Josh," she finished desolately.

"It's only for a little while," he said, squeezing her hand. "Just until word comes through from your father. You'll be able to come back then."

"Do you believe that, Josh? Really believe it?" She scanned his face anxiously.

"Of course I do," Josh's gaze did not waver.

Jenny sighed and felt the tightness ease out of her scalp. Her nervousness about the journey abated. The only anxiety she was left with was about the weather.

"Don't worry about it," said Josh firmly, as he walked back with her to Mariners Terrace. "It was fine yesterday. And it's fine today. At this time of the year we very often have a week or ten days of good weather. 'Fools' Spring' they call it."

"Do they? Well perhaps it *will* last then. Especially for us," Jenny remarked with a wry smile. It was her first attempt at a joke in six days.

Jenny felt a fraud. People kept popping in with little farewell-gifts for her to take to Canada. She had a telescope from the Blocks, a box of draughts from the Gochers, and a packet of butterscotch from Mrs McQueen and Meg. Even old Granny Fulcher hobbled round with a bottle of Mother Seigel's Syrup, which she said was good for seasickness.

The person Jenny most hated deceiving, however, was Mr

155

Hanley, because he was so obviously upset about her being sent away. He arrived at the door at ten o'clock on Monday morning with a small parcel for her.

"Two books by Robert Louis Stevenson, that you might find helpful," he said. "*The Amateur Emigrant* and *Across the Plains*. He was writing about his journey to America. But I should think you will find experiences in common with him."

Jenny felt her face grow red. "Thank you, Mr Hanley," she said politely. "It's very kind of you."

"And, Jenny, do keep in touch with me," he went on earnestly. "I will want to know what conditions you are living under, and how you are being treated. You must insist that you be allowed to write regularly to your friends. For if you are unhappy, I may eventually be in a position to help you to come home."

He looked so miserable, that Jenny could have wept. "But, Mr Hanley, when my father comes home, he will make them bring me back," she said.

The curate's eyes slid away from hers. "Yes," he murmured, looking down at the step. Without raising his head, he patted her on the shoulder and turned away.

"He doesn't believe that my father is alive. I could see that well enough," Jenny told Josh that afternoon, as they walked along the track to Godwit's. "I thought I might have depended on him, too."

"Grown-ups don't listen to children. Haven't you learned that yet?" said Josh. "I mean if your Aunt Clara had announced that she had this strong feeling that your father was alive, I bet they would have listened to her! That's why Godwit is so special," he added, his tone softening. "He has always listened to me."

"This will be the last time I see him," said Jenny, swallowing hard.

"Until you come back," Josh pointed out.

Jenny nodded, glad of Josh's strength. Without him at her elbow, keeping her spirits up, she would have been in floods of tears during these past few days. She had been in two minds

156

about making this visit to Godwit. The old man knew nothing about the plan to send her to Canada, or even about Jenny's father being missing, because Josh had said that the slightest worry nowadays drove him to the bottle. So it was going to be an unspoken, one-sided good-bye, with Jenny having to hide her feelings as best she could.

When they reached Godwit's door, however, she found that even that was to be denied her. There was a paper pinned to it, with the word 'Sleeping' scrawled across it.

"He hasn't been drinking again?" Jenny asked Josh in dismay.

For answer Josh led her round the corner of the house, then, with a sigh of relief, pointed to a large tin bath sitting beneath the kitchen window.

"No. It's all right," he said. "He must have been out eel-catching all night. I forgot the season had started. Sorry, Jen! You won't see him after all."

"Will you tell him what has happened, and where I am?" she asked, looking sorrowfully up at Godwit's window as they started back along the track.

"Yes. But I'll wait for a few days. Until I'm sure you are safely settled in Glasgow. There won't be anything for him to worry about then. I'm going to give you the address of my last school, Shrublands House," he added. "You can write to me there, as though you thought I was still a pupil. They'll send the letter to me inside one of their own envelopes, and no one at home will suspect anything, if they see it. I'll say it's from an old chum."

Jenny was beginning to feel nervous again. "If only the weather's as good as this tomorrow!" she said shakily, gazing across the browny-green flats to where the river sparkled in the sunshine.

"It will be," said Josh. "I feel it in my bones. Don't you worry. Nothing will go wrong, Jenny Wren."

Yet it almost did. That evening, when Josh arrived at Aunt Clara's door with the Gladstone bag, he was pink-cheeked and agitated-looking.

"Father's just flown into one of his tempers," he told Jenny, as he followed her upstairs and into her room. "He hasn't been in the best of humours anyway, because Margot's infant hasn't arrived, and Mother's going to be away for longer than she thought. Then he suddenly spotted Grandfather's *Manual of British Birds* lying under my bed, and did he blow his top! Said I had no respect for anything. Made me out to be a kind of grave-robber."

"Oh, Josh!"

"That didn't bother me particularly," Josh said, sitting down on the bed and mopping his brow with a dusty-looking handkerchief. "I mean I *know* that Grandfather wouldn't mind me having his book. What did worry me was when Father said I had to stay in my room all day tomorrow as a punishment! He meant it, too. I had to really grovel to make him change his mind, and to pretend I was heart-broken at not being able to sail *Roller*. I even squeezed out some tears. It was disgusting. Yach!" He made a noise as though he were going to be sick.

For the first time since they had started planning her flight, Jenny felt a stab of apprehension on Josh's behalf. What if it were discovered that he had helped her to run away? What would happen to him? He would never tell them where she had gone to. She was certain of that. And Mr Gale would be furious.

"Josh," she said, shaking his arm. "Are you quite sure that you want to go through with this? I mean, if your father ever finds out . . ."

"Oh, Jenny!" he shouted crossly, as he hurriedly began to shove the belongings she had laid out on the bed, into the bag. Then he turned round and grinned at her. "Actually," he said, "I'm quite beginning to look forward to it. It might be the most exciting thing I have ever done. And before I forget," he added, fishing a small brown purse out of his pocket, "here's the money. Just twopence short of three pounds. The address of the school is in there too. You had better keep that in a pocket, and not in the bag."

As Jenny took the purse, she opened her mouth to thank

Josh and tell him that she would pay the money back. But seeing Josh looking so young, standing there, she paused, a lump rising in her throat. He was almost as young as Samuel Block, yet of all the people she knew, he was the only one who had been prepared to fight for her. She had to turn her head away quickly, so that he wouldn't see the tears that were pricking at her eyes. By the time she had recovered herself, he was ready to leave.

"Nine o'clock. Don't be late, Jenny," he called anxiously from the landing.

"I'll be there," she promised with a sigh.

Later that evening, as Jenny sat at the kitchen table sewing pearl buttons on to the camisole Aunt Clara had made for her, a new worry came to torment her. What effect would her running away have on Aunt Clara? Would it make her ill again? She cast a furtive glance at her aunt sitting on the other side of the lamp, the warm light making her face softer and younger-looking. She did not mean to be unkind, sending her to Canada. Jenny knew that. Aunt Clara really believed in Mr Brightway and his Scheme. And the Waspes had convinced her that it would be the best solution, both for herself and for Jenny.

"But I have to think of myself and Dad," Jenny told herself firmly. "I must fight for our happiness. I don't want to harm Aunt Clara. But it just can't be helped if I hurt her a little."

"That's the way!" commented Aunt Clara approvingly. "You're gittin' handy with yer needle, Jenny. That's suffin' I've bin able to do for you at any rate."

Jenny raised her head and looked across at her aunt. "You've done a lot for me, Aunt Clara," she said earnestly. "I'm grateful. Truly, I am."

Aunt Clara made no reply, but she coloured and smiled as though she were pleased. Jenny hoped that, in the days ahead, her aunt would remember what she had just said.

Before supper Jenny ran round to thank the Blocks properly

for her telescope. She would see Leila, Mrs Block and the baby tomorrow morning, but probably not the others. So it was a kind of farewell visit. Following Mr Block into the kitchen, she found the scene little changed from that first occasion, when she had called on the family with Aunt Clara. Charlie and Robert were kneeling on the floor, playing marbles. But, as before, Lizbeth and Samuel were leaning against their mother who was just about to put Lucy to bed, and Leila was sitting darning at the table.

Realizing afresh how she was going to miss them all, Jenny's voice was husky as she said her thank you's.

"That's all right, my darlin'," said Mrs Block brightly. "That'll give you suffin' to do aboard ship."

"You'll have to look out for porpoises an' icebergs, an' warn the captain, do you see any," Mr Block told her jokingly.

As she wished them good-night, Jenny made a brave attempt at a smile. (Had she really been setting off for Canada the following Monday, she could not have held back her tears.) But, of the children, only baby Lucy smiled back. The three boys looked at her with sorrowful faces. Lizbeth wept openly on her mother's shoulder. And Leila was biting her lip hard.

Did Mr and Mrs Block really feel as cheerful as they looked, Jenny wondered. Or were they pretending in order to keep her spirits up? You could not tell with grown-ups. They tended to band together when a major problem arose. And it was true what Josh said. They did not listen to children then. Only to one another. She could well imagine that Mr and Mrs Block might have been talked around by the Waspes and Aunt Clara.

Queasy with nerves, she could not eat any toast for supper, and could drink only half a cup of cocoa.

"You feelin' all right, gel?" Aunt Clara asked, peering at her. "You look flushed to me. Don't say you've caught suffin', just when you're due to go away!"

"I'm tired. That's all," Jenny said, feeling irrationally hurt by her aunt's obvious anxiety to be rid of her to Mr Brightway.

In fact, by the time she had laid out the clothes she was to travel in next day – her turquoise dress, pinafore, coat, tam-o'-shanter, stockings, clean underwear and boots – she was indeed so tired that, as soon as her head touched the pillow, she slipped into a deep, dreamless sleep. She was wakened by the boatyard-bell jingling impatiently, telling her it was seven o'clock.

Chapter 19

They might have been going up the river on one of their usual jaunts, the way Josh sat grinning so calmly at her as she came scurrying along to the landing-stage, still crouched low in case any of the boatyard-workers spotted her.

"Down here in the stern!" he said quickly, pointing to a place in the bottom of the boat where a yellow oilskin lay. "Those are father's old oilies. You can pull them round you. We're going to have a strong following wind, so we'll be skimming along pretty nippily."

Jenny made herself as comfortable as she could, drawing her knees up and keeping her head down so that it did not show above the gunwale. *Roller* rocked gently, and every now and again her sail flapped as though she were anxious to be off.

On one side of the centreboard-case was the Gladstone bag, on the other, a dilapidated-looking picnic-basket containing food for them both, which Josh had filched from the larder. Josh was covering these with pieces of oilskin, whistling cheerfully, and showing no sign of nerves. Jenny envied him his coolness. She pulled her tam-o'-shanter down over her ears and hugged herself in a vain attempt to stop shivering. She had been shaking all morning, walking around in a kind of trance, so that she was now quite unable to remember what she had said to Leila in the baker's, or to Mrs Block over her cup of tea. She wished she could have left a note for Aunt Clara, telling her not to worry, but Josh had said that would only raise the alarm.

She watched Josh jump lightly on to the landing-stage and untie first the stern line, then the painter, keeping hold of the latter until he was back on board. Then, having coiled the lines away in the bow, he grabbed an oar and shoved off. The next moment he was sitting just above her, his right hand on the tiller, his left hand pulling in the rope he called the 'sheet'.

"Farewell and adieu to you, fair Spanish ladies,
Adieu and farewell to you, ladies of Spain,"
he bawled loudly as *Roller* dodged in and out of the anchored craft. "If they see my lips moving, they'll think I am singing," he sang to the same tune, giving Jenny a playful prod with his toe. The breeze had whipped colour into his cheeks, and his eyes were bright. He looked like any carefree boy enjoying a sail.

When they reached the middle of the river, he did something to the centreboard and pulled on the tiller, so that *Roller* swung slowly round, and her sail stuck out on the right-hand side. Jenny felt a difference in speed and motion immediately. The tops of the masts of the anchored boats began to fly past. At the front of the dinghy there was now a noise like water chuckling over pebbles. And, more ominously, *Roller* began to live up to her name.

Jenny found herself having to swallow hard every few seconds. Finally she could keep silent no longer. "Josh!" she cried urgently. "Can I sit up for a bit? I feel terribly queer!"

Josh glanced down at her briefly. "Oh, crikey!" he exclaimed. "You *have* gone green! Yes. Sit up quickly. There's no one near us at the moment anyway. But if I shout 'Ship ahoy!' you will have to go down again."

She pulled herself up by the gunwale and sat on the thwart, taking deep breaths. Soon she felt better.

"It's because the wind's aft," Josh explained to her. "When you came out with Father and me, we were beating against the wind most of the time, so she didn't roll much."

"Never mind. If she races along like this, we'll be there in no time. That's a blessing," she observed cheerfully.

"Yes," agreed Josh. Then he glanced quickly over his shoulder.

It was the second time he had done that since Jenny had sat up. Was something worrying him, she wondered. Could it be those dark clouds that had appeared away in the distance? Surely not. The sky above them was still blue, with only tiny rags of white-grey cloud sailing across it. Gazing beyond *Roller*'s bow, she thought for a moment that she was looking at more clouds building up. Then she realized it was only the smoke from a train.

"Ship ahoy!" Josh called sharply as a barge laden with bricks came into view.

Jenny slid down on to the oilies, her mind now running on trains – not the train whose smoke she had just seen, which had come from Lowestoft, and was, at that moment, creeping into Newbrigg station – but the London train which she was to catch at Wenford. And the Glasgow train she would board at Euston. She must look for the third-class, 'Ladies Only' compartments. And how should she travel from Liverpool Street to Euston? Should she walk? Or should she use some of Josh's money for a cab? So engrossed was she in working out the details of her journey that although the dinghy was rolling as much as ever, she did not feel in the slightest bit sick.

Jim Blowers had leaped down on to the platform of Newbrigg station and was already through the ticket-barrier before the eight-thirty from Lowestoft had pulled to a halt. His sister-in-law had wanted to send a wire to Miss Lovett. But Jim reckoned that he deserved this treat, since he had had to bring the bad news in January. He drew his brother's telegram from his pocket as he strode along Wall Road, and read it for the umpteenth time since Bob's wife had thrust it into his hand that morning:

ARRIVED I.O.M. ROUND IRELAND 8 WEEKS.
JUST HEARD OF TRAGEDY DEC. 31. MAIL LEFT
WITH LOWESTOFT 'ROBERTA RITCHIE' TO
POST AT NEWLYN. HAD EXPLAINED POSSIBLY
NO CONTACT 2 MONTHS. SORRY IF WORRIED.
TELL FAMILIES. CATCHES EXCELLENT. BOB.

He could not wait to see their faces – Miss Lovett's, and the
poor little old mawther's – when he banged that down on the
kitchen table for them to read. There would be no fainting this
time, he reckoned. Not unless Ted's poor gel swooned with
happiness!

Jenny felt as if they had been sailing for hours, although she
could see from Josh's watch that it was only half-past nine. She
was sitting up on the thwart again and Josh was pointing
things out to her: the tree branches sticking up out of the
water, marking the edge of the mud; a heron fishing in the
distance; how straight he was keeping the long, foaming
wake of *Roller*. He was doing this, Jenny suspected, to stop her
thinking, because she had suddenly been filled by a terrible
fear at the idea of arriving in Glasgow tomorrow morning and
having to find her way to Mrs Harris's. She had not been able
to contain her panic. It had come spouting out of her in
near-hysterical, disjointed phrases.

"All right!" Josh had cried, glaring at her. "I admit it won't
be very pleasant. But will it be worse than sailing off to
Canada with the orphans?"

This had steadied her. And now he was being kind and
trying to divert her. Or was he trying to distract himself. she
wondered suddenly as she caught that furtive gesture again –
the quick, hunted glance over his shoulder.

She looked in the same direction and felt a tingling of
unease. Those black clouds were certainly catching up fast.
And the water seemed to have changed colour too. It was
yellowish now – not very pleasant-looking.

As though sensing what was in her mind, Josh called determinedly, "We must make as much headway as we can while the wind's with us. She's running beautifully at the moment. Ship ahoy! Brewery steam-barge. Be ready for the wash!" he added, as Jenny slipped resignedly on to the floor-boards again.

The wash from the steam-barge rocked Godwit's boat so violently that it woke him up. He groaned as he threw off the old coat that covered him and struggled into a sitting position. He had not meant to sleep until daylight. But he had felt so deadly tired after his night's eel-catching that he had not had the energy to row home. So he had decided to stay where he was, moored in the creek, and to have an hour's 'shut-eye'.

"An' now look at that bleedin' sky!" he grumbled to himself. "Suffin's brewin' there an' no mistake. Reckon I'd best git the owd tarpaulin' over me, an' sit it out."

But the next moment *Roller* went skimming by with Josh at the helm.

The old man gasped and rose stiffly to his feet. "Josh!" he cried as loudly as he could. "Ahoy, there! *Rol-ler!*"

His voice was lost in the gurgling of water beneath *Roller*'s forefoot, and the rushing of the wind. The dinghy passed out of sight behind the reeds.

"He ought to have that sail down with a sky like that," the old man mumbled, as he lowered himself on to his seat with a grimace.

Then he became aware of the stillness all around him, and of the reeds standing straight as soldiers beneath the darkening sky.

"Wind's died now. That's some bad sign," he commented under his breath.

After a moment he sighed, unshipped his oars, then began rowing hard out of the creek and into the main channel of the river.

"What has happened?" asked Jenny, pulling herself up on to the thwart.

They seemed to be moving slowly backwards and there was no longer a cheerful noise of chuckling water. Then she saw that the sail was slack and the sheet hanging in loops.

"Wind's gone," Josh told her. "We're not sailing any more. We're drifting with the tide. A squall's coming up, I think. It's what I've been afraid of. I'll lower the sail and row for shelter. You pull Father's oilies round you, Jen. I'm going to put my own on."

But he had hardly finished speaking when the black sky above them was fractured by zig-zagging lightning. There was a crash of thunder, then a noise like gravel being thrown against a window.

"Crikey!" muttered Josh, slipping down to shelter under Jenny's cape.

The rain battered their backs, its grey curtain cutting them off from the river. They might have been sitting under a waterfall.

Then as suddenly as it had started, the shower stopped.

"Quickly!" Josh cried, throwing the oilskin off and standing up. "We must . . ."

He stopped, gasping, as, with an ominous rushing, a gust of wind came tearing across the water. *Roller*, kicked sideways, sheered wildly, shuddered, then heeled over slightly and lay quiet. It began to rain again with slow, heavy drops.

"Hell's teeth! Now we're on the mud!" yelled Josh in exasperation. "I must heave her off before she settles."

He grabbed the oars, and, still on his feet, began to try to row them back into deeper water.

"Oh, it's no good," he gasped eventually. "I can feel her settling. I'll drop the sail and unship the rudder. Then we'll both have to get out and rock her. Take your boots and stockings off, Jenny, and hitch up your skirts, and whatever you do, don't leave hold of the boat!"

Jenny did what she was told without question. One look at Josh's white face told her how serious the situation was. As she

166

swung her bare legs over the side, she realized that the rain had finally stopped and the sun had broken through.

The mud felt like soft rubber and was so cold that it made her feet ache.

"All right?" called Josh from the other side of the dinghy. "One, two, three . . . *rock*!"

She tried to copy Josh, throwing her weight on the boat's stern, then leaning back and hauling it up. But her right hand lost its grip on the gunwale and she almost overbalanced, her arm flailing wildly. Out of the corner of her eye she saw something bright make an arc through the air. Then she became conscious of her right wrist feeling oddly bare.

"Oh, no! My bracelet!" she wailed, looking behind her to where Josh's Christmas gift lay glinting on the mud a few feet away. "Wait a moment, Josh! I can't lose that!"

"Jenny! Don't leave hold!" Josh cried shrilly.

But it was too late. She had already started to flounder across the mud. Suddenly her right leg sank, thigh-deep, into the black ooze. Her left followed. She tried to struggle out only to find the mud was already round her waist.

"Josh!" she screamed. "Help me!"

"Throw yourself back!" he yelled. "Spread your arms wide. Look up at the sky. I'm coming. Don't panic!"

She did as he told her. But she could not help panicking. Her legs were like lumps of concrete, immovable, no matter how she struggled to raise them. And the mud was still sucking her under. She could feel herself going down very slowly. If Josh did not come quickly she would die.

"Josh! Help me!" she sobbed.

"It's all right, Jen! It's all right!"

By rolling her head slightly to the right, she could see Josh's white, anxious face. He had worked his way round the dinghy, and was now holding on to the gunwale with his right hand, while in his left he brandished an oar.

"Don't move," he called to her. "But when I hold this oar out to you, grip the end with both hands and cling on like the devil! I'm going to pull you out."

When the oar slid within her reach, she clutched it as though she would never let it go. "Pull! Now!" she screamed to Josh.

She could hear him groaning and gasping as, again and again, he pitted his strength against that of the mud, first using his right hand, then his left. Finally he burst out angrily, "Oh, this is hopeless, single-handed!" And, a moment later, there was a small, shocked cry.

The oar, suddenly heavy, tumbled from Jenny's fingers. She craned her head back to find that her worst fears were confirmed. Josh was now in the same predicament as herself, waist-deep in the ooze. Dry sobs shook her as she stared despairingly up at the mocking blue sky.

"We must call for help, Jen!" Josh shouted to her in a trembling voice. "It's our only hope. Shout. Together!"

Their cries were so thin they might have been those of two curlews.

No one will ever hear us, Jenny thought desolately. We're going to die. She was not consciously crying, but her face was wet with tears.

It seemed an eternity later, though in fact it must have been only minutes, that a voice yelled, "Hold on, there! I'm-a-comin'!"

She heard Josh's sob of relief. "Jenny, Jenny!" he cried. "It's Godwit! Godwit's come to save us!"

Presently she could see the old man, lying flat on the mud, propelling himself slowly towards them. When he reached the oar that Josh had dropped, he held it out with two hands in front of him.

"You listenin' now?" he called urgently. "I'm a-goin' to haul Jenny out first, 'cos she's sunk in deeper. I want you to git two hands round the middle of this oar, gel, like you was a monkey hangin' from a branch. Understand? Hold on as tight as ever you can an' I'll do the rest. When you feel yourself begin to come up, wriggle yer legs. That'll help some."

Jenny saw the oar sliding towards her, with Godwit's knobbly old hands clamped round it, wide apart. Her fingers curled round the wood.

"Hold tight, Jen!" Josh called encouragingly.

She heard Godwit groan deeply. For a moment she thought her arms would be wrenched from their sockets. Then she felt herself moving. She could wriggle her legs. Now she could lift them. Inch by inch they came up to the surface. Suddenly she could see them lying on the mud – two black sticks.

"Don't sit up," Godwit warned her. He was breathing in great gulps. "Jest lie as you are. I'm now goin' to pull you across to the boat."

She slithered along on her back, looking wonderingly up at the blue, cloud-speckled sky. She was alive. She was not going to die. She kept trying to thank Godwit, but each time she was choked by a sob. Then she was lying on the firm mud beside Godwit's boat, listening to her heart banging in her ears as she watched the old man wriggle back across the ooze towards Josh.

Five minutes later Josh and Godwit lay beside her, gulping for breath, and making groaning noises. Jenny found she was able to sit up. She put her hand on Godwit's shoulder.

"You saved our lives. Thank you! Thank you!" she cried, then began to weep, shivering and gasping.

Godwit smiled and squeezed her hand.

Gradually the noise of laboured breathing abated. Josh and Godwit pulled themselves up into sitting positions. Josh, with a smothered sob, hugged the old man tightly, then rose to his feet and looked miserably down at Jenny.

"I'm sorry," he said, biting his lip. "It looks as though we'll have to go back."

They were both black from head to toe, plastered with the stinking mud.

"It wasn't your fault," said Jenny, wiping away her tears. She was alive. For the moment that was all that seemed to matter.

"You *will* have to git back. An' straightaway," said Godwit breathlessly as Josh helped him to his feet. "Else you'll both catch yer deaths. Yer dinghy's stuck there till high tide by the looks of her, Josh. You'll have to come with me. I'll jest move that owd sack of eels. Then you can climb in."

As he stepped into his boat, the old man suddenly turned towards them, hand upraised. "Listen!" he whispered. His eyes were glowing.

A sound like a foghorn came floating across from the opposite bank. Or was it a bull bellowing? Once. Twice. Three times.

"If that ain't owd Bottlebump!" he said exultantly. "That make me feel like doin' a dance to hear that!"

Still smiling, he seemed suddenly to crumple. The next moment he lay in a small, still heap in the bottom of the boat.

"Fatal heart attack. He's beyond my help," said Dr Buchan gravely.

Josh flung himself against Jenny and began to sob as though his chest would burst. Every time he drew in his breath, his pain went through her like a knife.

"We thought he had fainted," she whispered to the blur of people in front of her. "He pulled us out of the mud. He saved our lives."

"The strain's been too much for him. His heart's probably been in a bad state," the doctor said.

They had been seen making their slow way down the river. Two children, filthy and distressed-looking, rowing a marsh-boat, with a body lying between them. Word had passed from sailing-vessel to anchored vessel, and finally to the quay. Boats came out to meet them, to bring them in to Field's landing-stage, where Dr Buchan and Police Constable Lewis were waiting at the front of a small, apprehensive crowd.

"Who is it?" a woman at the back called.

Josh turned on her. "It's Godwit Morley," he shouted fiercely. His anger was not against her, but against himself. His eyes were streaming. Between sobs he said indistinctly, "It's my fault he's dead." Then he turned and clung to Jenny again, moaning and shuddering.

Gentle arms encircled their shoulders and led them away.

Kind voices spoke above their heads. (One of them Jenny recognized as Bulldog Block's.) But all the time Josh's terrible crying went on and on without a break. On and on. Jenny stumbled along beside him, holding his hand, knowing there was nothing she could say to comfort him.

Chapter 20

Jenny stood at her bedroom window on Friday morning clutching her letters to her chest. Dark, fat clouds were racing across a grey sky, and a flock of gulls were sitting on the marsh, beaks pointed towards the wind. Josh had told her that the old fishermen believed the souls of men who were lost at sea became gulls and followed their boats home. She would have liked to think that was true. Not only of fishermen. She would have liked to think that Godwit was still somewhere out there. But of course it was not true. It was superstitious nonsense. Wicked nonsense, Aunt Clara would say.

The thought of Godwit brought a lump to her throat again. But her grief, painful as it was, could not detract from the happiness she felt as she looked down at the letters in her hand. When the postman had given her the three letters an hour before, and she had seen the handwriting on the envelopes, she had felt as though her heart would burst with joy. Two were from her father – one was for Aunt Clara, one for herself. The other, which was addressed to Jenny, was from Mrs Harris. She had put Aunt Clara's letter on the dresser, before opening her own and devouring their contents. Then she had sat down to read them both over again. Twice. Slowly. So as to really enjoy them.

Mrs Harris had not written because she had lost their address. It had turned up that very morning, she said, in her brother's old writing-case, and goodness knows what it was doing there!

"I couldn't even remember the name of the town, Jenny, my pet. My head's been birling like a peerie with all the upset of the removal. We lost the first flat we were after and had to wait for another in the same road, which was where we wanted to be. But now we're comfortably settled here in Parkview Road, so I'll be writing regularly. And hoping to hear from my own wee lassie, of course."

Jenny thought how she, too, might have been in Parkview Road by now, and for a moment did not know whether to feel sad or happy that she was not.

Her father's letter began with anxious questions. Had they believed the *Good Hope* had gone down with the other Lowestoft boats? Had they been terribly worried? Had they given up hope? Bob had decided, on the spur of the moment, to set off for Ireland (which had turned out to be the best move they could have made). The crew had all written letters home, explaining that they might be out of touch for a couple of months (for Blowers had found from past experience that trying to send mail from remote parts of Ireland was more trouble than it was worth). But of course all their letters had been passed over to the skipper of the ill-fated *Roberta Ritchie* and had gone down with the boat. A dreadful business! The news of the tragedy had made the *Good Hope*'s crew feel quite guilty, because they were so happy about the record catches they had made off Ireland.

"But life must go on. We're off up to Scotland now, and I'll see you in two months, darling. I never stop thinking about you and planning for our future which looks quite bright now," he wrote.

Jenny knew what her father meant when he talked of the *Good Hope*'s crew feeling guilty about being happy. That was exactly her own case at the moment when she thought about Josh. He had taken to his bed on Wednesday and refused to leave it, or to eat anything. Nothing that anyone said or did could comfort him, it seemed. Mr Hanley had tried to make him understand how much better it had been, both for Godwit and Aunt Clara, that the old man had died a hero, instead of squalidly, in a drunken stupor, as he might well have done. And on Wednesday evening, Mr Gale had hired a cart, driven it along to the look-out tower, and, with Jenny's help, had carried all Godwit's injured birds from the Shepherd's House, to transport them to the scullery of Galaxy House. But when he had begged Josh to come down and have a look at them, the boy had shaken his head and turned his face to the wall.

"Such terrible grief!" Mr Gale had whispered in a scared voice to Jenny. "If it goes on, I shall have to wire to his mother to come home."

Jenny had had Aunt Clara to worry about too. On Wednesday morning, shortly after Jenny had been brought home from the river, Aunt Clara had burst into the kitchen, followed by Jim Blowers. She had thrown her arms about Jenny, mud-plastered as she was, and held her tight for several minutes before she told her the good news about her father. The tears had been running down her cheeks.

"If anything had happened to you, whatever would I hev told yer father?" she had sobbed.

Jenny had not known whether she ought to confess to Aunt Clara that she had been running away to Glasgow. She asked Mr Hanley what he thought, when he came in to see her on Wednesday afternoon, for she had no hesitation in confiding in him. She felt that he remembered what it was like to be a twelve-year-old and in a muddle.

"No, my dear. Don't tell her," he said immediately. "Don't tell anyone else. Josh isn't talking at the moment. But I'll warn him, too, when he feels better. Field's men have brought *Roller* back. I'll go down and fetch the bag for you, and you can unpack your belongings before your aunt comes back from work."

"I thought . . . but isn't the truth always best?" Jenny stammered.

"Not in this case," Mr Hanley replied. His tone was kind,

but firm. "Miss Lovett must be skating over some pretty thin ice at the moment. Emotionally, I mean. If she thought she had failed you so badly, she might go under. As it is, she has a chance – now that her poor father has redeemed himself in the eyes of the town – of feeling she is free at last. Am I making sense? Do you understand me, Jenny?"

She did, in a hazy sort of way. Yet it was more by instinct that she did the right thing that evening, when she found her aunt sitting crying quietly in the parlour, with the photographs of old Mr and Mrs Lovett, and of Alfred, on her lap. Jenny sat down beside her, rested her head on her shoulder, and told her, in as great detail as she could, how Godwit had saved Josh and herself from the mud. When she had finished, Aunt Clara gave a long, shivering sigh, squeezed Jenny's hand, and said quietly, "Thank you, gel." Although Jenny could not know it, with those three words Clara Lovett made her peace both with her natural father and with Newbrigg. Just before they went to bed that night, she said suddenly to Jenny, "Do you know, Jen, I fare to think I might go out to Canada myself an' help with Mr Brightway's children in the Reception Centre. He did say they needed a good cook. I'd wait till yer father and you were gone, of course."

"Well, I hope she do!" Mrs Block said fervently on Thursday morning when Jenny repeated this to her. "I truly hope she do! An' I hope she meet a good, kind husband as well. Clara deserve some happiness."

Jenny heard Mrs Waspe use almost the same words that evening when Aunt Clara confided to her friend what was in her mind. But Mrs Waspe's tone was somewhat different from Mrs Block's.

"You certainly deserve to find happiness, Clara," she said sternly. "But I hope you realize the implications of what you intend to do. Starting afresh in a strange country at your age! Is it not risky?"

"I'm not afraid, Harriet," Aunt Clara replied placidly. "I'm goin' to write to Mr Brightway before the week's out. I've decided."

Mrs Waspe's disapproving "Tut!" was quite audible to Jenny, who was about to climb the stairs. She doesn't like Aunt Clara striking out on her own, thought Jenny, feeling first indignant, then amused. She could not resist tiptoeing over to peer through the crack in the door at Mrs Waspe's discomfiture.

Jenny was sure now that she had no need to worry any more about Aunt Clara. But what about Josh? If she could only think of something to say or do, to break through his wall of grief! But he refused to look at her, or to speak to her. Mr Gale had taken her in to see him several times to no avail. Poor Mr Gale! Jenny had never imagined she would ever feel sorry for him. But she did now. The last couple of days had made him haggard and ill-looking. He had told Aunt Clara that he could not possibly go to work until Josh was better. And, although he was so worried about the boy, he had insisted on making the arrangements for Godwit's funeral tomorrow. He had determined that Godwit was to go in one of the Gale burial-plots, and not into a pauper's grave.

Jenny looked miserably out at the pewter-coloured sky. Poor little Josh! She had not realized just how much the old man had meant to him. He had probably loved Godwit more than anyone in the world. And what could you say to someone who had lost the person they loved best?

"Jenny! Jenny!"

Jenny jumped. To begin with, she could hardly believe it. But, yes, it was Josh calling her from downstairs.

She ran out on to the landing. "I'm here!" she cried. "Wait! Don't go away!"

"I won't. I have something to tell you," Josh said. He was standing just inside the front door. Although he looked skinnier than ever and chalky-faced, his dark-ringed eyes shone up at her.

"What?" she asked, running down to him.

"Father's bought me the North Marsh." His voice trembled slightly.

"What!"

"The North Marsh. For a bird sanctuary. He offered more than any of the property developers. I'm going to change its name to Godwit's Marsh. A kind of memorial."

"Oh, Josh!"

"And there's something else. Do you know what Father told me this morning? Grandfather always blamed him for the boating accident. Father had promised to go out with the other four that afternoon because he was the most experienced yachtsman. But he cried off and went to meet Mother instead. That was before they were married. Grandfather never forgave him. Poor old Father! Wasn't that rotten for him, Jen?"

Jenny nodded. What had meant more to Josh, she wondered? Being given the North Marsh, or his father confiding in him?

"Oh, and Margot's baby has hatched at last. A girl. Virginia Charlotte. What a mouthful!" Josh suddenly blinked hard and looked away.

Jenny knew then that the battle between happiness and grief was still going on inside him. She waited for him to recover.

"Uncle Josh! Old Uncle Josh!" she said, gently teasing.

He turned red and grinned self-consciously. "Another female. Catchpole's curse," he observed, pretending to sigh. Then he looked at his watch. "Must dash," he said. "I promised to go down to the lawyer's with Father. About the Marsh, you know. Can you come out this afternoon?"

"I expect so," said Jenny, smiling.

She walked out to the road and stood looking after Josh as he ran home. A figure appeared, striding towards him. It was Mr Gale. The two met. She saw Mr Gale ruffle the boy's hair. Then Josh slipped his arm through his father's and the pair walked companionably down the hill towards the High Street.

FRYING AS USUAL
Joan Lingard

Disaster strikes the Francettis when Mr Francetti breaks his leg. Their fish and chip shop never closes, but who is going to run it now that he's in hospital and their mother is in Italy? The answer is quite simple to Toni, Rosita and Paula, and with the help of Grandpa they decide to carry on frying as usual. But it's not that easy . . .

THE FREEDOM MACHINE
Joan Lingard

Mungo dislikes Aunt Janet and to avoid staying with her he decides to hit the open road and look after himself, and with his bike he heads northwards bound for adventure and freedom. But he soon discovers that freedom isn't quite what he'd expected, especially when his food supplies are stolen, and in the course of his journey he learns a few things about himself.

KING DEATH'S GARDEN
Ann Halam

Maurice has discovered a way of visiting the past, and whatever its dangers it's too exciting for him to want to give up – yet. A subtle and intriguing ghost story for older readers.

STRAW FIRE
Angela Hassall

Kevin and Sam meet Mark, an older boy who is sleeping rough up on the Heath behind their street. Kevin feels there is something weird about Mark, something he can't quite put his finger on. And he is soon to discover that there is something very frightening and dangerous about Mark too.

JUNIPER
Gene Kemp

Since her dad left, Juniper and her mum have had nothing but problems and now things are just getting worse – there are even threats to put Juniper into care. Then she notices two suspicious men who seem to be following her. Who are they? Why are they interested in her? As Christmas draws nearer, Juniper knows something is going to happen . . .

THE SEA IS SINGING
Rosalind Kerven

Tess lives right in the north of Scotland, in the Shetland Islands, and when she starts hearing the weird and eerie singing from the sea it is her neighbour, old Jacobina Tait, who helps her understand it. With her strange talk of whales and 'patterns' Jacobina makes Tess realize that she cannot – and must not – ignore what the singing is telling her. But how can Tess decipher the message?

RACSO AND THE RATS OF NIMH
Jane Leslie Conly

When fieldmouse Timothy Frisby rescues young Racso, the city rat, from drowning, it's the beginning of a friendship. It's also the beginning of Racso's education – and an adventure. For the two are caught up in the brave and resourceful struggle of the Rats of NIMH to save Thorn Valley, their home, from destruction.

A TASTE OF BLACKBERRIES
Doris Buchanan Smith

The moving story about a young boy who has to come to terms with the tragic death of his best friend and the guilty feeling that he could somehow have saved him.

TUMBLEWEED
Dick King-Smith

Sir Tumbleweed is tall and thin with bright red hair and a droopy moustache. Not surprisingly, life in Merrie England is pretty dull for this ordinary knight when he's so nervous and accident-prone – he practically trips over his own suit of armour! But the flattering attentions of an evil-looking witch, a lion and a unicorn change his life and before he knows what's happening he has floored Sir Basil the Beastly in a jousting match!

MR MOON'S LAST CASE
Brian Patten

Mr Moon is old and tired. He's had enough of this life but he still believes in magic. Something stirs in his soul when he hears there have been reported sightings of a strange, child-sized being, called a leprechaun by the press, and he decides he must track it down. A long journey begins and as his obsession with finding the creature grows, he is carried to the brink of fairy-land itself.

MYSTERIES OF THE SEALS
Rosalind Kerven

All the fish have disappeared from the waters around the Scottish fishing village where Tom and Katie live. There is something sinister happening. The men have all been laid off and the whole village seems to be falling asleep – it's almost as if someone has put an evil spell on the place.

GAMES . . .
Robin Klein

A ramshackle, eerie and isolated house, set on the fringe of the Australian bush, seems an ideal venue for a weekend party to Kirsty and Genevieve – particularly when the owner, Kirsty's aunt, is known to be away. Poor Patricia Miggs, more of an afterthought than a friend, tries desperately to win their approval now that she has the honour of their company. However, the fears that she holds for her lack of social graces are as nothing compared to the sheer terror that engulfs all three once the party is abandoned and the games begin . . .

COME BACK SOON
Judy Gardiner

Val's family seem quite an odd bunch and their life is hectic but happy. But then Val's mother walks out on them and Val's carefree life is suddenly quite different. This is a moving but funny story.

AMY'S EYES
Richard Kennedy

When a doll changes into a man it means that anything might happen . . . and in this magical story all kinds of strange and wonderful things do happen to Amy and her sailor doll, the Captain. Together they set off on a fantastic journey on a quest for treasure more valuable than mere gold.

ASTERCOTE
Penelope Lively

Astercote village was destroyed by plague in the fourteenth century and Mair and her brother Peter find themselves caught up in a strange adventure when an ancient superstition is resurrected.

THE HOUNDS OF THE MÓRRÍGAN
Pat O'Shea

When the Great Queen Mórrígan, evil creature from the world of Irish mythology, returns to destroy the world, Pidge and Brigit are the children chosen to thwart her. How they go about it makes an hilarious, moving story, full of original and unforgettable characters.

COME SING, JIMMY JO
Katherine Paterson

An absorbing story about eleven-year-old Jimmy Jo's rise to stardom, and the problem of coping with fame.

BOY and GOING SOLO
Roald Dahl

The enthralling autobiography of this much loved author, from his earliest days to his experiences as a pilot in the second world war.

THE APPRENTICES
Leon Garfield

A collection of the much-acclaimed Apprentices stories. Each story features one London trade and is linked by recurring characters.

THE BONNY PIT LADDIE
Frederick Grice

Set in the early 20th century, this story of a boy growing up in a mining village was one of the first children's books to show real working-class children in credible surroundings.

SARAH, PLAIN AND TALL
Patricia MacLachlan

What would she be like, this new mother found through a newspaper advertisement? And above all, would she be able to sing?